GOOD NEIGHBOURS

by Frank Sol

Copyright 2011 Cosmic Legends Publishing

Drafts2Digitial Edition, License Notes

This book is licensed for your personal enjoyment only. This book may not be re-sold or given away to other people. If you would like to share this book with another person, please purchase an additional copy for each recipient. If you're reading this book and did not purchase it, or it was not purchased for your use only, then please return to your favourite retailer and purchase your own copy. Thank you for respecting the hard work of this author.

This is a work of fiction. Names, characters, places, and incidents are products of the author's imagination or are used fictitiously and are not to be construed as real. Any resemblance to actual events, locales, organizations, or persons, living or dead, is entirely coincidental.

Content warning: For adult readers over the age of 18 only. This book contains explicit sexual situations between two men.

The characters portrayed are of legal age for sexual consent within Canada.

Chapter One

Sean finished hanging his fishing gear up on its appropriate hooks in the garage. Everything had been rinsed off or otherwise cleaned up and then neatly organized. *'Buy good quality gear when you start out. Don't just buy something cheap unless you really only plan to use it once. Look after your gear and you won't have to replace it every year.'* That was the advice his father had given him when they first started going on fishing trips.

With a grunt, Sean reached down and picked up the bag containing what few extra clothes he had taken along, and the small bag of leftover groceries he'd brought back with him. He triggered the garage door and ducked out under it before it had a chance to finish closing. The chain was making a loud groaning sound.

"I'll have to get that looked at soon," Sean muttered to himself. He'd been saying that for weeks now, but always never quite got around to making a call. Stifling a yawn, he walked up the short sidewalk to his front door.

The townhouses lined along the street all shared pretty much the same design in looks and layout. Inside and out.

'The cookie cutter approach,' his co-worker, Sylvester, had announced one night after they had been drinking at an office Christmas party. *'When you drive home late at night, how do you know which door is yours? What happens if you go into the wrong place and crawl into someone else's bed?'*

'Well, if he's cute enough if won't matter...' And they had both laughed at that.

Sean gazed off down the street. His unit was on the very end of the row, so he only had neighbours on one side to worry about, a fact he liked immensely. Even though it was late afternoon, there was no one else in sight. That was a little unusual, given how warm the late spring day was, but the silence was still nice.

Almost like still being out on the lake, he thought with a tired, though satisfied, grin. *All things considered, I'd still rather be fishing.*

After enjoying a comfortably warm shower—one aspect of a weekend away fishing that he did miss—Sean dressed in some comfortable lounging clothes. The loose track pants and tee-shirt were both loose, well broken-in and very comfortable. He'd tossed his clothes into the washing machine and it was chugging away softly.

Returning to the kitchen, he poured himself a good stiff drink—his preference was rum and coke, on the rocks—and then he took a seat in his favourite chair. The rocker had belonged to his grandfather, having been custom-built for him, and it had been the one possession that Sean had requested as a keepsake after the old man passed away. He rocked slowly, savouring his drink. *What better way to end a Sunday?*

He leaned just far enough forward to pick up his *Kobo* ereader from the coffee table and returned to the novel he'd started reading last Friday.

A loud rumbling motor drew his attention to the living room window.

A green *Mazda* was pulling into next door's driveway.

That's not Jacob's car, he thought in surprise. *Is he having company?* He made an effort to see exactly who had pulled up. Some of the visitors who stopped in next door were quite hunky. *Maybe I should get myself a job as a contractor.* Getting to hang around those muscular, well-built construction workers would likely have some fringe benefits. *Plenty of material to fuel my late-night fantasies,* he thought. *And that wouldn't be a bad thing. Why, if Jacob had any idea just how many times he's been featured in one of my late night jerk-off sessions, he'd probably—*hello!

It definitely wasn't Jacob getting out of the *Mazda*.

Jacob wasn't six feet tall.

This guy was.

Staring through the window, Sean licked his lips. *Hello indeed.* He sighed softly. The man had a nice face, with a square jaw and a long nose. *A Roman nose*, he thought to himself. The man stepped away from the car, and Sean could see how his pectoral muscles made his black tee-shirt bulge. Lower down, toward his waist, the fabric hung down limply over the waistband of his shorts.

The man was well proportioned, with nicely shaped legs showing beneath his denim shorts. He walked around to the trunk and popped it open. He bent over, and his cotton tee-shirt rode up, exposing his back. It was his head of salt-and-pepper hair—mostly salt—which really made Sean's cock twitch in his track pants.

I do have a thing for grey-haired men, he admitted. *That moustache looks nice too. I bet it would tickle when it rubbed across the right places.* The man wore the dusting of five o'clock shadow quite well too.

Sean forced himself to blink.

The man slammed the trunk closed with his right hand, and then carried the grocery bags up to the door of Jacob's house. He paused on the step just long enough to fish some keys out of his front pocket and let himself in.

Sean sighed softly and let his hand slowly drift down to the crotch of his track pants. '*Down boy,*' he told his swollen dick, not that it made any difference. *That is just one walking wet dream!* He thought about going over to introduce himself. *Play the role of a good neighbour out to see what's going on.* Then, just as quickly, he decided it really wasn't any of his business. *I'm not going to go over to Jacob's and make a fool of myself over a guy,* he told himself. *That's not my style.*

No matter how hunky the guy was.

But tonight in bed, he thought. *Oh tonight, all bets are off.*

* * *

"Hi, can I offer you a drink of some kind?" Sean gave his new neighbour as friendly and inviting a smile as he could manage.

"Sure." He nodded his silver-haired head. Seen close up, his square-jawed face was lined and showing signs of age, but the effect made him looked ruggedly handsome. "That would be real nice."

"Good. Why don't come inside with me?"

Sean climbed the stairs to his door and pushed it open—he could the hear the other man's shoes on the steps behind him. Stepping inside, he held the door so his neighbour could enter.

Up close, he could see just how well the man's wide shoulders filled out the thin cotton shirt he was wearing. The top few buttons were open, hinting at his hairy chest. He let his gaze drop down so he could check out the way his neighbour's ass filled his blue jeans.

The man turned around.

Sean quickly dragged his gaze away from the man's crotch and back up to his face. "The kitchen is just through there," he said, waving his hand distractedly.

"Okay. After you."

Sean brushed past him, close enough so he could *accidentally* bump against him.

As soon as they were in the kitchen, Sean turned to face his guest. He could smell his clean scent—a strong soap with faint hints of cologne and sweat—and he inhaled deeply. He stared into the man's brown eyes, and felt his own mouth mimic the man's ready smile.

"Welcome to the neighbourhood," Sean told him.

"Thanks." The man took a step closer, a grin on his face and a twinkle in his eyes. "I'm enjoying it so far."

"You'll find that it has a lot to offer."

"Oh, I have no doubt about that." He held up his right hand and then began to run it slowly across Sean's chest.

Sean returned the favour, still staring dreamily into those blue eyes, before he finally raised his hand to caress one of those stubble-covered cheeks.

The man turned his head and kissed Sean's palm.

Sean blinked, startled, but quickly regained his mental balance and lifted his other hand to gently pull the man's head towards his.

His lips were half-open.

An instant later, their mouths met, their arms encircled one another, and they kissed passionately.

They finally broke apart.

Sean grunted. He'd lost all track of time in that sweet, and seemingly endless, kiss. *Is this really happening?* he wondered. *Did I really just grab this guy off the street and lure him into my house to have my way with him*

The man was smiling at him.

Fuck yeah I did! Sean thought.

"Do you want to fuck me?" the man asked.

"Hell yes!"

"Then do it."

Without another word, Sean grabbed the man's hand and pulled him deeper into the house.

Sean led his guest into the bedroom. He left the door open and pulled his guest close so they could kiss again.

The man returned the kiss with passion and strength.

Sean's hands dropped to the front of the man's jeans.

"Stop, let me." He gripped Sean's tee-shirt at the waist with both hands and slowly pulled it away from his shorts. As he raised it, exposing Sean's stomach, he bent and began to kiss the bare flesh that was uncovered.

Sean shivered and groaned. The man's kissing had reached his nipples and now he took one into his mouth, flicking his tongue slowly over it. Sean squeezed his eyes shut and tilted his head back, his mouth opening in a soft moan of pleasure. He lost track of exactly how long both of his nipples were teased.

The neighbour lifted his mouth away so that he could finish pulling the tee-shirt off and over Sean's head.

Sean opened his eyes.

His neighbour pushed him gently backwards and he fell onto the bed.

Staring up at the ceiling, Sean felt a warm hand fumbling with the drawstring of his nylon shorts. As it was slid down his legs, his hard-on sprung free and to full erection. He could feel sticky dampness on his stomach and he knew he was leaking.

"I'm really enjoying what this neighbourhood has to offer," the man said.

Sean looked up to see his neighbour standing and looking down at him.

He was smiling. "You've got a fine body." He bent forward, extended one of his big hands and began to stroke Sean's chest once again.

Sean couldn't suppress a powerful shiver. The feel of the man's hand on his chest when felt through his tee-shirt had been sensual, the actual feel of his warm hand against his bare skin was intoxicating.

The man looked down at him again. "Enjoying it?"

"I'd enjoy it more if you were naked too."

"Well then...." The man reached for the front of his shirt and ripped it open—one of the buttons bouncing off of Sean's chest—and then casually pulled the remains from his back and shoulders, letting it drop to the floor. He unzipped his jeans and pushed them—and his underwear—down his muscular legs.

"Fuck me," Sean gasped.

"Maybe in a bit," the man said. His cock was fully aroused, sticking out in front of him. He climbed onto the bed and lowered his mouth onto Sean's dick.

Sean dragged his hands across his neighbour's bare back, feeling each and every steely muscle. The feel of those lips wrapped around his shaft made him groan, the tongue gently teasing his sensitive cock-head.

The pressure increased. The man was riding up and down Sean's shaft, licking and sucking like a pro.

Sean gasped as he came, shooting his load before he had fully registered how tight his balls had become.

A soft slurping sounded as the man swallowed.

Sean slumped against the bed, gasping. "Holy shit, that was amazing."

His neighbour lifted his head and smiled. "I'm glad you liked it."

Chapter Two

Monday morning dawned far too early for Sean's taste.

Especially after such a hot fantasy during his late night masturbation session.

Yawning, he made a mental note to buy more baby oil—he was just about out—and then his eyes closed again.

Finally—three snooze cycles later—he pushed back the covers and rolled out of bed. Bleary-eyed, he pulled a dark green terrycloth robe around himself before stumbling into the bathroom to sponge himself off, and then staggered downstairs to the kitchen.

"I can spend the weekend getting up at the crack of dawn to go out on the lake and try to catch fish and yet getting up at seven to go to work is a chore." Still muttering, Sean sipped his refilled mug of *Earl Grey* flavoured tea. He needed two cups at least before his brain would finally awaken fully.

Taking another sip, Sean walked through the living room and pulled open the blinds. The rising sun poured through the window, making him blink. Getting his eyes to stop watering, Sean looked towards his next door neighbour's driveway.

The green *Mazda* was still in Jacob's driveway.

Sean frowned at the sight. *The hunk must have spent the night there,* he thought with a trace of envy. *He might still be asleep...or showering right now.* His dick twitched under his bathrobe and he mentally gave himself a quick shake. *No time for that kind of thinking right now.*

Sean took another drink of his tea. There was no sign of Jacob's own *Toyota* though. *Where's his car? It can't be in his garage... you couldn't fit a bicycle in there.* He knew full well that Jacob had so much junk crammed into his garage that there was no room for anything else.

Maybe Jacob's car is in the shop for repairs. That could be a loaner car, but that doesn't explain who the guy was.

Glancing at the clock ticking away on the mantle, Sean shrugged and headed to his bedroom to finish getting dressed for work.

* * *

A day spent going over monthly accounts was no match for a day spent fishing.

Not by a long shot. Sean scratched idly at a bug bite on his neck as he fired up his computer. *Damned mosquitoes are already out...and it's only May.*

His inbox beeped loudly. A string of emails was waiting for his attention. One of them was from Zach Morganstern, the firm's owner, looking for volunteers to attend some upcoming tax conference.

"I went to the last one." Sean shook his head at the thought of attending another one this year. Even with expenses covered, it wasn't worth going. *Those things are as boring as hell.* The only fun came from getting away after hours to go clubbing or else some other pre-arranged meeting. *Or if you go with some hunky co-worker.* He'd read plenty of online stories about guys who attended out-of-town conferences and ended up sharing a hotel room with a co-worker which always led to wild sexual romps—and, of course, kept secret from the rest of the office and the inevitable wives back home.

Sean stared at the message again, giving it some thought, then shook his head. *No, thank you.* This particular conference was just for one person to attend and he didn't feel like dealing with the every day busyness of Toronto. *Let someone else have the fun of going. Eric maybe.*

"So, did you land a big one?"

"What?" Sean looked up, startled at the sudden question.

Jackie was standing in the doorway, a smile playing across her face. She had her brown hair neatly coiled into an intricate braid, and the neckline of her pale yellow top was cut just low enough to hint. Her navy blue skirt and jacket were both cut to show style. "I just asked how your fishing trip went. Why are you blushing?"

"Too much sun this weekend," Sean replied. He could feel his cheeks flushing—for some reason, he was thinking of the hunk with the *Mazda*. "Just a bit too much sun."

"I don't know how you can enjoy that," Jackie said as she stepped into the office. "Hours and hours just sitting in a boat holding onto a stick."

"Well you know what they say about a man and his stick."

"It's all in the wrist?" Jackie laughed with him. "It's not my idea of amusement." Not by a long shot."

"Fishing's not for everyone. I like it."

"Good for you."

Sean chuckled. "You went to Toronto for that concert, right?"

"Yes."

"How was it?"

"Fantastic. You should have gone with us."

"Maybe next time." Personally, Sean had no desire to accompany the office staff on a three hour road trip to watch a long-past-their-prime country band play songs he'd hated listening to as a kid when he father controlled the radio.

"Your loss."

"I know." Sean gestured towards his computer. "I hate to cut you off, but I have a lot of work to catch up on."

"I knew it! Too much time last week daydreaming about fishing and not enough working." Jackie gave him a conspiratorial wink and a grin. "I won't tell the boss on you." Still grinning, she turned to leave.

Sean shook his head.

* * *

Sean backed into his driveway and parked his silver *Ford Focus*. He left the radio playing until the catchy song ended—he no idea who sang it or what it was called, but he liked the beat—then opened the door and climbed out. He lifted his arms over his head and stretched before reaching for his briefcase.

Too long hunched over that damned computer, he thought. *I need a nice hot shower and a full body massage.* He could get the shower inside at least. *How do I find someone for that massage?* It was just too much effort to go looking online for someone.

A loud rumble drew his attention away from the door and he looked down the street.

That green *Mazda* was back.

The day is looking up, Sean thought. *I've got some eye candy to enjoy.*

The *Mazda* pulled into Jacob's driveway and the growl of the motor died. The door opened and the hunky stranger got out. He was wearing a red tee-shirt and thin green nylon shorts this time. "G'day, Mate!" he called out, waving his arm.

"Good afternoon," Sean replied, returning the wave. The man was Australian—no mistaking that accent for anything else. Leaving his briefcase on the front steps, he walked across the driveway.

The other man waited for him to approach.

He is even nicer close up, Sean thought. *Yes, quite the hunk. Just like in my dream.* He really liked that silvery hair; it made the man look distinguished. The man's square-jawed face did have some lines, but the overall effect was one of rugged handsomeness which made Sean's knees grow weak. "Hi, I'm Sean Dupel." He held out his right hand.

"Jamie Fletcher."

"Nice to meet you." *Jamie has a nice firm grip,* Sean thought as they shook. *I wonder how firm his grip would be on other things?* He felt his cock twitch inside his slacks at the thought and he forced himself to keep eye contact. *However much I want to undress you with my eyes.* "You staying with Jacob?"

"I'm looking after the place for him." Jamie reached around to scratch his neck and his tee-shirt lifted slightly. The inches of bared flesh were tanned and hairy. "He was called out of town to look after some big project."

"He mentioned he was doing some work on some big mansion." Sean nodded his head as the memory resurfaced. "New lottery winner going overboard or something."

"Yeah, something like that. A bloke and his shelia and their ankle biters."

Sean blinked, trying to sort the slang. *Wife and kids?*

"He's expecting to be away for a few weeks. Maybe a month or more. Has that big renovation conference in Toronto in a few weeks too."

I love your accent. Sean knew that he was grinning like a fool. "I recall him mentioning something about that at his barbeque last month." He had been far more interested in catching glimpses of some of the construction workers at that party than in listening to Jacob talk shop. *Not that any of my hints or gambits scored any hits. Those guys were all straight or totally uninterested.* "So you're looking after the place for him?"

"Yep. He offered to let him stay here while he's away. I need a place for a few months."

"Just visiting Canada then?"

"Yeah, how'd you guess?" From the grin on his face, Jamie already knew the answer.

"Your accent is pretty noticeable."

"I guess it is." Jamie shrugged. "Actually, I'm thinking about moving over here. Got a permit and all that government shit to work here. Might try for full status and citizenship eventually."

"Good luck with that," Sean told him.

"I'm gonna try it for a while first."

"So...what do you do?"

"Brickie."

Sean shook his head, his eyes widening. "I'm no wiser."

"Bricklayer."

"Ah. So you're working for Jacob?"

"Yeah, he's helping sponsor me."

"I wish you luck with that."

"Thanks. Now I should take this stuff inside before it melts." Jamie bent to retrieve a grocery bag from the back seat of the *Mazda*, and the sight of his butt cheeks straining against the thin fabric of his shorts made Sean's heart—and his already semi-hard cock—leap.

"I'll leave you too it then. Nice meeting you." Sean tried to will his cock to settle down before it became too noticeable. It was a lost battle though.

"You too, mate." Jamie walked around to the front door of his house.

Sean hurried across the driveway to his own house. He had the fly of his slacks unzipped and his hard cock out and gripped in his hand before the door finished closing behind him.

Staggering into the living room, he dropped onto the blue chenille couch. He quickly unzipped his pants and reached into his briefs. He wrapped his fingers around his hard shaft and began stroking himself vigorously. He closed his eyes and tilted his head back, squeezing his eyes shut so he could visualize Jamie's face.

"Oh, god, " he moaned as he pumped himself. *Jamie was just so hunky in appearance. What I wouldn't give for just a few minutes alone with him. Especially if he was naked and willing to play!* His body suddenly stiffened, and he cried out. "Ahhhh!" With a final spasm of his body, he felt himself cum, jets of white liquid shooting out of his cock and splattering across his blue dress shirt.

Panting, Sean looked down at himself. "Well damn," he mumbled.

Rising to his feet, he stumbled towards the bathroom.

Chapter Three

Dressed in just a loose pair of silk boxer shorts and a grey tee-shirt, Sean wandered through the house. The stereo was playing some music—soundtracks on random shuffle—which gave a nice relaxing feel to the morning. Taking a sip from his second cup of *Earl Grey* tea, Sean glanced through the living room window.

Jamie's *Mazda* was parked in the driveway.

I never heard him come home, he thought in surprise. The car had been gone when he had first gotten out of bed that morning.

Jamie must have gotten the muffler fixed.

Damn. How the hell was he supposed to sneak glimpses of his hunky neighbour if he couldn't hear his car coming and going?

Sean shook his head at the absurd thought. *What am I?* he wondered. *His personal stalker?* After a moment, he to admit the answer was probably *yes.*

And I'm okay with that, he thought. *It's been a week and I've still only managed the single conversation with him.* Jamie kept odd hours, coming and going really early or else really late. *He can't be working all that late at night? What does he do with himself?*

A stranger, new to the country...he might be lonely and looking for friendship.

And possibly something more? Sean wondered hopefully.

Sean was on his third cup of tea when he heard a truck noisily pull up across the street.

Frowning, Sean hurried from the kitchen to the living room window to see what the rattling was.

There was no mistaking the dark purple coloured pick-up and heavily-laden trailer. *Flat Earth Landscaping* had finally worked their way down to his end of the street. He looked to the right, but Jamie's car was gone again.

Missed him again!

Sean watched as the three men in the landscaping crew got out of their pickup truck. *Men!* They were college-aged at best, but all three were in fine shape. They were talking quite animatedly amongst themselves as they worked to get their equipment unloaded.

One, in a red shirt and black jeans, dropped the back flap of the trailer and rolled a mower down the ramp. Sean was familiar with him—the man was in his twenties and had been around for two years or so.

Another, in a green tee-shirt and blue jeans, grabbed some clippers and headed around the back of the duplex. This guy was new—Sean hadn't seen him before this year.

Good for him, Sean thought. *I guess that* Flat Earth *must doing well if the owner can afford to hire more staff.*

The third, the oldest of the trio, pulled his baseball cap lower, to better shade his eyes. He looked briefly towards Sean's house, then turned and lowered the trailer's ramp. Taking one of the lawn mowers, he headed to the back of the house.

Sean licked his lips and sat down in his rocker. *Now I get to enjoy an hour or so of amusement,* he thought. *I'm so glad I don't have to go into work today.* After having put in extra hours all week on a big case, he was supposed to just stay home and relax. *Friday off, and then the rest of the weekend. Wish I had known about getting this Friday off sooner...I could have gone fishing again.*

Of course, he quickly noted to himself, he still could load up his fishing gear and take off on a day trip at least.

Tempting, he thought. *Very tempting. Nothing around here to keep me in town. Why not take off again?* He glanced back out of the window. *Well, once the show's over with that is.*

The sound of lawnmower engines broke the silence.

Hey, this counts as relaxing, Sean thought as he watched the landscapers working on Janet McMichael's yard.

Red-Shirt finished mowing the front lawn—it was only a few square metres after all—and left the mower beside the truck. He moved onto the low hedges which lined the front porch. He had picked up a pair of pruning shears from the trailer and was cutting away the dead growth.

The day was getting warm—the sun was already quite hot, hinting at the summer to come—and before long, the red tee-shirt was damp with sweat.

Green-Tee-Shirt emerged from the backyard, dragging a plastic garbage can filled with branches he had trimmed. His shirt was dark with sweat as well.

Sean sighed. *I could make you boys sweat,* he thought to himself. *Just come on over and give me a few minutes of your time.*

Sean stared out through the living room window.

The man in the red tee-shirt was standing by the end of the driveway wiping the sweat from his forehead.

Poor man, Sean thought. *He looks so hot and worn out.*

Sean walked to the front door and swung it open. "You look hot!" he called out. *In more ways than one, that is.* "Can I offer you something cold to drink?"

"Sure." Red-Tee-Shirt had a deep voice. He walked towards the house.

Sean stared, then tore his eyes away from the hunk before his rapidly stiffening dick would become noticeable. *Luckily this tee-shirt is baggy enough to hide the bulge.* And his silk boxers would pass for shorts. "Come on in." *Fuck, he has great legs.* "Would you like water or lemonade?"

"Anything is fine. Thanks."

Sean brought a tall plastic glass from the kitchen. "The lemonade is fresh. Old family recipe." He watched Red-Shirt take a long swallow from the glass. *He has such nice legs,* he thought. *So muscular.*

Red-Shirt lowered the glass from his lips. He drained half the glass.

"I don't envy you working outside in this heat."

"It's not so bad. Better than being out in a blizzard. You just get used to it, learn to pace yourself."

"Oh, well I'm still impressed." Sean gave Red-Shirt as friendly a smile as he could manage. "You want some more of that?"

"Yes, thanks."

"I'll get it." Sean could hear Red-Shirt following him down the hall towards the kitchen. *Now or never, right?* He turned around. "Can I be blunt with you?" he asked.

"Yeah."

"I want you to fuck me."

Red-Shirt said nothing.

Sean kept the smile on his face. "I've been watching you for years...you're totally fucking hot and I want you so badly I can barely restrain myself from ripping your clothes off right here and now."

"Okay."

Sean's smile got wider. *He's not running away!* "I want you to fuck me senseless."

"I can do that."

Sean set the glass onto the counter. "You are—" he broke off as Red-Shirt grabbed him and ripped his grey tee-shirt open. *I thought I said I was gonna rip* his *clothes off?* A moment later, his silk boxers were yanked down.

Sean was pushed backwards another step, stumbling as his feet snagged inside his boxer shorts. He felt himself start to fall, then Red-Shirt caught him and lowered him onto the kitchen table.

Red-Shirt kicked off his work boots, pulled his own tee-shirt over his head and then tossed it onto the counter. He undid his belt, then his fly, and let his denim shorts drop on to the floor. His dick was already half-erect.

Sean rolled over, positioning himself face down on the tabletop, stomach flat on the oak, his own hard-on dangling off the edge.

Red-Shirt ran his hands down Sean's back, then pulled his ass-cheeks apart.

Sean gasped as he felt a tongue rimming him.

Red-Shirt's tongue lapped at Sean's ass, dipping his tongue in and out. He didn't make a sound.

Sean grunted and moaned, giving a fully audible appreciation of how much he was enjoying the other man's efforts. He looked back over his shoulder as the rimming stopped..

Red-Shirt had stood up. He was hard, his dick at full attention.

Sean opened his mouth to—

—and Red-Shirt shoved his hard-on into Sean's ass.

Sean cried out and his fingers tightened on the edges of the table.

Red-Shirt pounded him, his cock plunging deep into his ass, and he felt the table shaking from the force.

Sean grunted helplessly as the other man rode him. He'd never had someone fuck him so furiously before. He clenched his ass muscles more tightly, squeezing Red-Shirt's dick. His own hard-on was thumping against the underside of the table.

Red-Shirt continued to thrust his cock into Sean's tight asshole, obviously enjoying the pressure on his dick.

Sweat dripped onto Sean's back. The table was thumping against the wall. He couldn't believe the sensations he was experiencing.

Shoving himself as deep as he could manage, Red-Shirt, finally, made a sound. A deep guttural cry as he finally came and shot his load deep into Sean's ass.

Sean cried out as he shot his own load across his legs and onto the floor. He slumped onto the table, gasping.

Red-Shirt pulled his dick out.

Sean lifted his head and turned it to look.

Red-Shirt had picked up the torn rags of Sean's grey tee-shirt and he was using it to wipe himself off. "Did that meet your expectations?" Red-Shirt asked as he began to get dressed.

Pulling his boxers back up, and then staggering across the kitchen to lean against the counter, Sean blinked his eyes tiredly. "Fuck yeah." Sean nodded.

"Fuck yeah...." Still panting, Sean gave himself a shake and sat up straighter in the rocking chair. *Flat Earth's* pick-up truck was driving off up the street and the front of his silk boxers were wet and sticky. "I've got to stop doing stuff like this," he told himself with a grin. *Some day someone's gonna walk in the door while I jerking off and then....*

Chapter Four

"So, here's where you're hiding yourself. Hard at work I see."

Down on his knees, Sean looked up from the flowerbed and a warm smile quickly spread across his face. It matched the sudden warmth flooding his loins.

Jamie was standing in the driveway.

"Afternoon, Jamie. I'd offer to shake hands with you but...." He held up one of his muddy hands.

Jamie walked closer and looked down at him. He was holding a coffee mug in his left hand. "Looks like fun actually. I'm no bludger, afraid of getting my hands dirty. Nothing wrong in working up an honest sweat."

"Yeah, I agree." Sean licked lips. He was kneeling, and thus his eyes were at the perfect level to stare directly at the other man's crotch. The blue denim jeans were dusty, as was his dark green tee-shirt. He had to consciously remind himself to look up towards Jamie's face. *Not staring at his crotch!* "Yard work...the perils of living in a mini-community like Limestone Markets. They have rules we all to follow."

"So what are the rules for lawn care?" Jamie asked. "I mean, it's part of my being here. Looking after Jacob's place, I mean."

Sean stood up and dusted his hands together. It didn't help to dislodge much of the dirt. "Well, the front has to be kept neat, as you can see." Sean gestured to the row of houses along both sides of the street. "Grass should be kept short—but it's not like anyone goes around with a tape measure checking—and it's supposed to be watered enough to keep it green. The community has a contract with a local landscaper which looks after any of the major yard work. We pay a bit less in fees if we do stuff on our own though."

"I'd wondered about that."

"They were here this morning—you might have seen them around here this week. *Flat Earth Landscaping*, with a purple pick-up." He shrugged. "Which was sufficient encouragement to send me venturing out here and try my hand at taming the wilderness before it overtakes my entire yard.

"Oh." Jamie shrugged. "I was out running errands. I must have missed them then."

"Yeah." *I saw that your car was gone. You came back and went inside while I was in the bathroom taking a leak.* He'd been sorry to have missed seeing Jamie come home from work. *He's definitely been working hard—you can tell from his clothes. I wonder if he'd notice me brushing close enough to get a good smell of him right now. The results of a good honest day's sweat and all.* "Jacob usually mows his own yard. The mower is in his garage, if you can find it."

"I'm trying to avoid the garage," Jamie admitted. "I think he did it last Saturday morning. Before he left."

Sean nodded. The lawn did look like it had been recently mown. "You can't have any large trees in the front, but we can put shrubs along the house and sidewalk."

"I don't think I'll be going to that extent," Jamie said with a laugh. "I'd think I'm limited to just 'mowing as needed.'"

"It's still early in the season yet for needing much mowing. You should be good for a few weeks. Unless it rains a whole lot."

Jamie gestured towards Sean's house. "I like the roses curling along that wall."

"Yeah, roses are my favourite flowers."

"And what do you like in the back?" Jamie asked.

"I prefer not to talk about the back," Sean replied a bit stiffly.

"Something to ashamed of? An oversized log perhaps?" Jamie walked around the side of the house, towards the gate. "I'm sure it's nothing that a little *whacking* can't fix."

"Well...."

Jamie looked around, his head swinging from side to side. "Wow."

"Yeah, it got a bit overgrown." Sean shrugged. "I haven't been home much on the weekends to really make a dent in this."

"I gathered that."

"I like to go camping and fishing. Get away from the city."

"Looks to me, mate, like you could save a few bucks by just going camping out here in this jungle." Jamie chuckled.

Laughing with him, Sean had to agree—the back yard was rapidly turning into a total jungle. "I haven't been home much to work on it," he protested. "I'll have it beaten back into shape eventually though. I like to entertain in the summer."

"Yeah, it's great to be outdoors." Jamie was smiling—he had two little dimples which added to his cuteness. "It's winter back home, you know."

"I thought so."

"I got to enjoy my own summer, and now I'm here to enjoy yours."

Sean shared his smile. "You'll have to come over for a barbeque."

"I'd like that. I'll bring a plate with me." Jamie eyed the backyard again. "Can I help you beat off?" he asked.

Sean's jaw dropped open.

"Beat the yard into shape, I mean."

"Oh, well if you want too." Sean coughed into his hand. "I won't turn down another helping hand."

"That's good to know."

"Can I offer you a beer or something?" Sean asked. They'd been out in the garden working for a couple of hours at least. He glanced at his wrist, but he'd left his watch inside. *A good few hours,* he thought.

Jamie straightened up with a tired groan. He wiped the worst of the dirt from the knees of his jeans, but they clearly showed the results of a day spent in the garden. "Yeah, mate, that would be great." He'd taken the shears and cut back the bushes in the back yard. He'd gathered quite a pile of brush.

"I can get the hauled off to the depot," Sean explained. "The city has a drop-off for yard waste. It all gets mulched or something."

"That's good to know. Be a damned shame to just landfill this."

"The city tries to be green. I think we do a good job with recycling and stuff." Sean went into his kitchen. He rubbed the front of his track pants—he'd been sporting a hard-on for most of the afternoon. *Watching Jamie bending and working is almost too much for me,* he thought. *I'll need to some serious stroking in the shower after this.* He thought about dashing off to the bathroom for a few minutes to relieve some tension, but decided he shouldn't really disappear for that long.

He carried two beers back outside.

Jamie was still down on the grass. He had discarded his sweaty-soaked tee-shirt.

Sean almost missed a step on the stairs. He managed to get down from the porch without mishap and handed a cold beer to his helper.

Jamie took a long drink from the bottle.

Sean took a swig out of his own bottle. *Oh my God!* His body was amazing.

Jamie's chest was smooth and muscular. His arms were big and he looked extremely fit. And he was tanned all over—no tee-shirt tan.

Oh my God! Sean thought again. His hard-on was getting even harder now. He hoped his hanging tee-shirt would cover its presence.

"This is really good," Jamie told him. "I was looking at the beer store earlier, but had a hard time trying to decide what to buy. Now I know this brand is good."

"It was my dad's favourite brand. So it's what I grew up drinking. When I was old enough to drink, I mean." Sean took another sip. "I usually drink rum-and-coke, when I want to savour something, but a cold beer on a hot day is really nice."

"That it is, mate. That it is."

Sean tried not to look.

Jamie had a decent bulge in the front of his jeans.

Is he hard or is that just natural? Sean took a drink. "Are you enjoying the neighbourhood?" he asked.

"Yeah. It's got a lot of charm."

"It's quiet—that's what I like the best. It's got a lot to offer."

"Right you are, mate." Jamie nodded his head. "I'm taking advantage of *everything* this neighbourhood offers me."

Sean's eyes widened. *Oh really?*

Jamie took another swallow from the bottle.

* * *

"Do you want another beer?" Sean called out.

"Sure, mate," Jamie replied.

Sean walked back into the living room. He handed over the beer, then sat down on the couch next to him.

"Would you believe that it's been over a month since I got a piece of ass." Jamie announced after a long drink. "I'm just not having any luck meeting anyone. I'm too shy I guess."

"You're shy?"

"Yeah." Jamie shrugged. "Just haven't met the right person."

"Are you looking?"

"Yeah."

Sean nodded his head. "Me too. No one special in my life right now. Hasn't been for a long time."

"So how long since you last scored?"

"Oh, I don't know."

"How long?" Jamie pressed.

"Six months. Maybe more."

"Six months?" Jamie's voice was loud and disbelieving. "Bloody hell, mate. You haven't gotten laid in *six* fucking months?"

Sean shrugged.

"Fuck." Jamie shook his head. "How do you go that long? I think I'd pay for an escort if I had to go that long."

Sean laughed. "I have porn and two hands."

Jamie's mouth hung open. "Bloody hell."

Sean smiled. "But it's more fun if another person is there." He let his hands drop down to the front of his pants and stroked himself openly. The thin nylon material of his trackpants showed off his bulge nicely.

Jamie licked his lips.

"Well...you interested?" Sean asked.

Jamie didn't hesitate at all. He stood up and unzipped his jeans. He let the denim drop to the floor.

Sean stared. His cock was just beautiful—its eight-plus inches was a nice thickness, the shaft was smooth, and the cock-head was well-shaped. He had a nice set of balls hanging down too.

"Does this answer your question?"

Sean pulled his tee-shirt off and quickly shoved down his trackpants and boxers.

They stood there for a moment.

Then Jamie let his hand rest against Sean's thigh.

Sean moved his own hand so that it was sliding along Jamie's thigh, almost touching his erect dick, until he was stroking his balls.

Sean dropped to his knees and took Jamie's cock into his mouth.

Jamie stumbled backwards a step, and ended up falling onto the couch.

Sean shuffled forward, He moved Jamie's leg, moving him into a prone position on the couch, so that he could once again lean forward. He grabbed Jamie's cock with his right hand and grasped his balls his left.

Jamie was wearing a big, encouraging smile.

Sean leaned in close—-Jamie's groin had a strong manly scent, the after effects of an afternoon spent labouring in the yard—and the muskiness made him even hornier. He began to lick Jamie's balls, while his hand stroked his cock with a slow and gentle motion.

He sucked on those balls for a good five minutes, maybe longer, and Jamie was moaning softly the entire time.

Eventually, Sean abandoned them to work his way along the shaft. He licked his tongue over its entire length, dampening every inch. Jamie's cock seemed hot to his touch, and once he got to the head he found it coated with pre-cum. The liquid was thick and sweet.

Sean continued to lick the shaft, teasing the hard-on with his mouth. He took the whole thing into his mouth.

His free hand was playing with Jamie's balls—he knew from past experiences just how good that felt when someone did it to him, and it always made him cum so much harder.

Jamie was moaning softly. "Just keep doing that." He was thrusting his hips upward at a faster and faster pace as well, giving in to his need to cum.

Sean grinned and pulled his mouth away. "Not so fast," he said. "I don't want this ending too soon."

Jamie opened his eyes. "You can't tease me like this."

"Do you ever top?"

"Fuck yeah!" He grinned widely. "You want me to cum inside you?"

"Yeah."

Jamie nodded and tried to sit up.

"Be gentle, it's been a while for me."

"Me too."

Sean positioned himself over Jamie's erection. "You ready?"

"Hell yes!"

"Here goes." Sean lowered himself until he could the cock-head pushing against his hole. "Do it!"

Jamie thrust his hips upward.

"Fuck!" Sean cried out.

"Should I—"

"Keep going!" Sean felt the brief pain recede. "Fuck me," he prompted. "Come on, Jamie."

"I'm not gonna be able to hang on for long," the other man gasped as he moved his hips in a thrusting motion.

"That's okay," Sean gasped. "I'm getting close too." He bent forward so that he could kiss Jamie's mouth. His own hard-on was trapped between them, and the friction of it rubbing was growing too strong to ignore for long.

Jamie's grin grew wider. He began thrusting faster, grunting with every push, and gritting his teeth.

Sean knew he wore much the same expression on his own face.

"Oh my God!" Jamie cried out.

Sean squeezed his ass muscles, and he felt the warmth inside him as his neighbour blew load after load of hot sweet cum into his ass. That was enough for him and he arched his back as he finally lost control of himself. "I'm—" he started to gasp, but fell silent as white goo erupted from his dick and splattered across Jamie's stomach.

Jamie slumped on the couch and Sean collapsed on top of him.

"God," Sean moaned. "I haven't cum like that in ages."

Jamie looked at him with a tired smile. "Glad that you enjoyed it," he said.

Sean could still feel the other man inside him. "Are you still hard?" he asked in disbelief.

"Yeah..." Jamie replied a bit sheepishly. "I told you it's been a long time."

"Do you want to cum again?" Sean asked.

"Can we?"

"Go ahead."

Jamie started moving his hips again. It was slower and far more sensual this time, the earlier urgency and desperation was gone, and now it was just two men enjoying the feel of each other's bodies.

Sean grunted and lifted his head. He'd barely gotten back inside the house before he was tearing off his sweaty tee-shirt and yanking down his trackpants to free his throbbing hard-on from the confinement of his boxers. He had jerked himself off furiously...desperate to work off the tension of being around Jamie all afternoon.

He had succeeded with that. The results were slowly cooling on his chest.

He scooped his boxers from the floor and used them to wipe off his groin and chest.

"Fuck," he muttered. "I really spurted." He had cum starting to dry on his face. He could feel it.

I could just go to sleep right here, he thought. *Close my eyes and wake up sometime late tomorrow.*

With a grunt, he forced himself to get back out of bed and staggered to the bathroom. *First a nice hot shower to wash away the sweat and dirt,* he told himself as he reached for the taps. *Then you can think about dinner.*

And laundry, he added to the list. The bedding needed washing.

Chapter Five

"So, I trust that you are aware of the upcoming conference in Ottawa?"

Sean nodded his head, in unison with Sylvester and Jackie. The break room was really just one of the smallest offices in the building, but well-equipped with a fridge, microwave, and a table and chairs. "Yeah, Eric. I saw the memo the boss sent around last week. It sounds really exciting."

Glaring at the others, Eric Hawkins shook his head. "You also realize that it is just going to be more damned paperwork for us to keep track of."

Sean eyed the other accountant over the rim of his coffee mug.

Eric was in his late-thirties and always very well dressed in expensive suits. He made full usage of the firm's gym membership, keeping himself trim and fit. He was six feet tall and maybe two hundred pounds. His face was handsome enough to warrant a second look—and most girls, and a few guys, usually did when they saw him.

What a pity he's just so damned full of himself, Sean thought sadly.

"Still, I guess that's why we have office assistants." Eric smirked at the others. "Well, why *some* of us do."

Sean managed to keep his own expression steady.

Jackie refilled her coffee mug. She stirred it with more vigour than usual.

"So I hear you were the chosen one," Sylvester said, putting his mug down on the counter.

Eric's mouth twitched.

"A week or so in Ottawa...should be fun. Once you get past having to actually do some work...without your assistant."

Sean tried, and failed, to keep a smile off his face. Sylvester was tormenting Eric and taking a very obvious pleasure in it.

Eric body stiffened. "I do plan to enjoy myself there. Plenty of opportunity to partake in some decent nightlife there. A large and cosmopolitan city like Ottawa tends to be considerably more eventful than around here." His tone had gone cold. "A week away from this place will make for a very nice change of pace as well." With that announcement, he turned and walked out of the break room.

"That wasn't very nice of you," Jackie said. She managed to sound stern...but then she began laughing. "But it was amusing to see him taken down a few pegs."

"Yeah," Sean agreed. "That it was."

They all laughed.

* * *

Sean parked his car in the driveway and got out. He looked at his own front door, and then deliberately turned and walked up the short sidewalk to the neighbouring house. He rang the bell, feeling a twinge of nervousness race through him as he stood there.

He was wearing his usual his regular work clothes—a pale blue oxford shirt, crisply pressed grey wool slacks and blazer, and a gold necktie. *I might be a tad overdressed for this,* he thought.

Jamie opened the door and looked out at him. Jamie was dressed in a plain black tee-shirt and faded blue jeans.

"Hi." Sean licked his lips. "I'm just on my way home from work and thought I'd stop in and see if you needed anything."

"Oh, I could use something. Come on in." Jamie turned and walked back into the house, leaving the door open.

Sean pulled the door shut behind him. Then he followed Jamie into the shadowy living room, enjoying the coolness of the inside air after the warmth of the day. The curtains were drawn most of the way.

Jamie turned around. "So you just thought you'd stop by?" he asked.

"Well, yeah."

Jamie took a step towards him. "I was hoping you would." Without another word, he grabbed Sean and pulled him into a tight embrace.

Caught off-guard, Sean hugged him back.

Just as abruptly, Jamie loosened his grip, but kept hold of Sean's hand. He pushed his guest onto the leather couch. Then he dropped down beside him.

Sean snuggled more tightly against Jamie's firm body. "Do you greet all your visitors like this?" he asked softly.

"Only the cute ones."

"So I should come by more often then?"

"I've been watching you."

"Oh?'

"Watching you staring at me. Every time I come home, you're in the window watching me walk across the driveway. If I'm in the yard, you find some reason to be out in your own yard."

"Yeah, I can explain that."

"You're stalking me."

"I should leave." Sean tried to swallow in a suddenly dry throat. "This was a mistake."

"Was it?

"I should go."

Jamie shook his head. "You ain't getting away that easy, you wanker."

The harsh growl took Sean by surprise. Then he felt Jamie suddenly grab at his tie and pull his face closer to his. Then he felt Jamie's lips pressing against his own in a kiss. *That moustache does tickle.*

Sean's hands dropped down to fumble at Jamie's zipper, managing to get the faded jeans undone while their mouths stayed locked together. His hand slipped through fabric and he felt Jamie's rock-hard cock. It was warm in his hand. He held the shaft for a moment, then slowly worked his grip up and down its length.

Jamie grunted. "You get into the bedroom," he ordered in that fabulous Australian accent. "Get naked. Now."

Sean managed to scramble to his feet. He knew the way through the house from previous visits—Jacob's house had the exact same layout as his own did.

Jamie followed him into the bedroom.

Sean paused.

Jamie licked his lips and gave a single nod. "Very nice." He undid Sean's tie and whipped it off, then unbuttoned his shirt, slipping a hand inside to pinch Sean's right nipple. His grin grew bigger when Sean jumped. "Like that, do ya?" He bent down and took the same nipple into his mouth.

"Yeah," Sean groaned at the feeling. He ran his own hands through Jamie's grey locks. The hair was thick, not greasy or lank, but nice to the touch.

"Get on the bed." Jamie pushed Sean onto the bed—Jacob's queen-sized bed—and then threw himself on top of the other man. They kissed again, Jamie pinning Sean down on the bed.

Sean struggled, though even he wasn't sure if he sought to free himself, or take the lead.

Jamie froze in mid-struggle.

"I thought I was supposed to get naked."

Jamie nodded his head, sat up, and began stripping off his tee-shirt and jeans. His tight briefs were bulging, the pale green material barely able to contain his hardness.

Sean quickly followed, throwing pieces of his suit to the floor.

Jamie came at him again, planting kisses all over Sean's body, working downward until he took Sean's cock in his mouth.

Propping himself on his elbows, Sean lifted his head and watched Jamie suck. Jamie was focused on his work, sliding up and down the shaft with tightly sealed lips, pulling Sean's balls just hard enough to tighten the skin on his shaft and further heighten his pleasure.

"I'm going to shoot if you keep doing that," Sean groaned.

Jamie stopped sucking and lifted his head. "Not yet, you're not. This load's for me, mate." He sat up and reached over to the nightstand. He pulled a tube of *K-Y* out and squeezed the lube out onto his hand.

Sean gasped as his felt Jamie's gooey hand begin stroking his cock. "Are you gonna jerk me off?" he gasped. The sensation of another man's hand on him was incredibly stimulating.

"No," Jamie replied. He reached behind his legs with his still lubed-up hand.

"Oh," Sean said.

Jamie pushed him flat on the bed again. Then he straddled Sean's body, his knees on either side of his waist, took hold of his cock again and positioned it between his cheeks. "You ready?"

"God yes." Sean felt his head pushing against Jamie's tight hole and then it slid in.

"Oh yeah," Jamie grunted. "Like riding a croc." His eyes were half-closed, his mouth hanging open, his face upturned with pleasure. "God, that feels so great," he whispered.

Sean moaned in agreement as he felt Jamie sliding up and down on him hard-on. He could feel Jamie's tight muscles clench against his skin.

Jamie reached down and pinched his nipples.

"Fuck!" Sean gasped and felt himself almost climax.

"Fuck is right," Jamie told him, grunting the words. "Fuck me harder, mate." He pumped himself more quickly up and down. "Fuck me 'til I can't walk!" He squeezed Sean's nipples again.

"I can't hold it!" Sean gasped. He'd hit the point of no return and cum rushed up from his balls and pumped through his hard-on. He cried out in pleasure.

Jamie literally screamed out as he came.

Sean felt hot liquid splash across his stomach and chest. He even felt some splatter on his face.

"Oh my God," Jamie slumped forward, Sean's dick slipping out of him, and he collapsed on top of the other man. "That was blooming amazing," he gasped.

"I've got no complaints on this end either." Sean was also gasping for breath. "I haven't cum that hard in months."

Jamie was smiling. "Glad you decided to be neighbourly," he said. He shifted position slightly, smearing the cum between their bodies.

* * *

"What a wild dream," Sean mumbled as he slowly opened his eyes the next morning.

It had certainly been an amazing dream...there was no doubt of that. No mistaking it either—the front of his silk boxer shorts were still a sticky mess. "Yech." He pulled the waistband out and looked inside. *Yep,* he thought, *major wet dream last night. I thought I was past having those.*

Just as he'd come awake, for a brief moment, he had been certain that he was going to roll over and find Jamie in bed next to him.

But it was just a dream.

He rolled out of bed and headed for the shower. Still wearing his boxers, he stepped under the spray, luxuriating in the feel of the water pounding against his skin. And the way in which the wet silk clung to his rapidly hardening cock.

"Wasn't once enough for you?" he asked aloud. Squeezing some body-wash gel into his hand, he took hold of himself and started stroking. The way he felt, it didn't long before he was shooting another load of cum across his stomach.

Chapter Six

Sean stood in the backyard, studying it. After Jamie's help, it looked a lot better, but there was still a lot of pruning and other chores to be done.

He heard a car pulling into the driveway.

Sean moved across the grass, stepping around some of the plants and trying to see.

It was Jamie coming home—he recognized the sound of the car—but he couldn't see anything from the backyard. The fence was high enough so that he had privacy, as did all of his neighbours.

"Damn it!" he cursed softly. *Wrong place, wrong time.*

He could hear voices.

Two of them. Sean frowned. He couldn't make out what they were saying, but one of those voices was definitely Jamie. *No mistaking that particular accent after all.* He tried to see, but the foliage and fence prevented him from seeing anything. *By the time I go through the house, they'll have gone inside probably.*

Sean gave himself a quick shake. *What are you doing?* he asked himself. *Seriously, what are you doing? You are stalking the poor guy. Next thing, you'll be sneaking across at night and staring through his windows like some pervert.*

Now that *was* a tempting thought, he admitted to himself. He knew which bedroom Jacob used and which windows looked into the two guest bedrooms. He could just slip over there and—

"What the hell am I thinking?" he asked aloud. "Christ, I've got it bad."

* * *

"I've got it bad," Sean admitted in a low voice. He darted a few looks around, but none of the other *Starbucks* patrons appeared to be paying any his conversation attention. They were all busy with their own, or reading papers, or studying the screens of ereaders and cell-phones.

"*You* fell *hard* for someone?" Leaning back in her chair, Rosemary looked surprised by the revelation. Her loose red top had sequins woven so it shimmered as she moved, though it clashed somewhat with her dark green skirt. "I thought you were past the whole 'love at first sight' idea. You were a lone wolf." She laughed.

Sean stared across the table at her. He reached for his coffee mug, sniffed at the concoction—Rosemary had ordered for them both and she had a fondness for triple latte things over plain coffee—and then took a sip.

She was still chuckling. "So Sean finally fell for a guy...does he know about you being in love with him?"

"No, of course not!"

"Does he know you're gay?"

"I don't think so."

"Is *he* gay?"

"I don't know. Maybe." Sean heard the desperate hope in his own voice.

"So you're lusting after a straight guy, luv?" She laughed even louder this time.

"Why do I confide in you?" Sean asked. He darted a few looks around at the other patrons but no one was really paying attention to the two of them.

"Because every gay man needs a fag hag."

"I thought you preferred the name *fruit fly*."

Rosemary shrugged. "Either works, luv." She ran her hand back through her short and spiky hair.

Sean had never had the heart to tell her that she looked like a caricature of an exceedingly butch lesbian. *One who went to the Tammy Faye Baker school of make-up application.* She could have been pretty, but the overdone make-up made her look cartoonish. Her being well on her way to three hundred pounds didn't help either. With a sigh, he turned and looked out of the window onto the mall parking lot.

"You need to find yourself a man you can actually obtain," she told him in a cheerful voice. "Of course, you *might* have a chance at this one." She took a long swallow of her own coffee. "Maybe I should come by and meet him. One or the other of us should be able to get him into bed."

Sean's eyes widened. "Are you in the market again?"

"Yes."

"What happened to Doug?"

"He couldn't ride the rocket long enough."

"Or Chris?"

"I caught him cheating with my last roommate. He was lousy in bed anyway. Too skinny for me really...I like a man with some meat on his bones. And a nice *boner*," she added.

Sean rolled his eyes. "Oh god."

"Relax, you're not my type, luv."

"Oh, thank god for that."

"Anyway, let's not talk about me. Or Doug. Or Chris and that tramp Nikki. And don't get me started about Victor...just don't go there."

Sean frowned. *Who the hell is Victor?*

Rosemary leaned forward. "I want to hear more about this Jamie guy. Pictures would be nice...why can't you buy a phone with a camera? Then I could see this guy for myself."

"I'm not a fan of cell phones, Rose. You know that. I just want a regular plain phone to talk on...I don't need something more powerful than my laptop."

She snorted. "Right...everyone says that, luv, until they get one. And then it's always 'how did I live without this'!" She tapped her own phone, then hastily shoved it back into her purse. "Talk about your stud-boy neighbour."

"There hasn't been all that much to talk about. He's just staying there right now until he finds a place of his own I guess. After Jacob gets back from his vacation and conference and whatever."

"So your time is limited. You need to make a move on him. Take him on a date."

"A date?"

"Well, a guy's night. Go bowling or bar-hopping or something. Invite him over to watch the game on the TV. Slip him a few drinks and then take him to bed."

"Rose!"

"What? You can always blame the alcohol." She was grinning widely.

"Is that how you get men to go to bed with you?"

"Yes."

Sean sat there with his mouth hanging open.

She looked back at him, a smug expression on her face, sipping her drink.

"I can't believe that you—"

"What? A girl's gotta do what a girl's gotta do."

"I can't believe I'm sitting here listening to this."

"Get over yourself, luv. You want him, go grab him. Or someone else will."

* * *

Standing beside his living room window, Sean watched the green *Mazda* start up.

Jamie was heading off somewhere.

Sean sighed. *I've got it bad for him,* he thought. *Dreaming about him at night, lusting after him by day, watching his every coming and going.* He had to do something about this growing obsession and soon.

But what?

'*Slip him a few drinks and then take him to bed.*' He heard Rosemary's voice clearly in his head. '*You can always blame the alcohol.*'

It certainly was a tempting thought.

I could call him back over to help with the yard again. Offer him a few beers as we go and then see where that leads us. I might be able to get him drunk enough to lure him into bed with me.

No, that was a bad idea.

"He'd probably take a swing at me." Sean gave himself a shake. "He's a bricklayer. One good punch would knock me flying." It would be a mistake to listen to Rosemary and try to lure his neighbour into bed.

"I'll just keep being neighbourly to him. Keep things friendly and non-sexual." That was the best policy.

Isn't it?

Chapter Seven

Sean drove up his *Ford* into the hills just a bit north of the city. The Little Cataraqui Conservation area had always been one of his favoured spots to go hiking. It certainly wasn't as fulfilling as going out past Buck Lake for a weekend-long camping trip, but it would do well enough to get him out of the city.

I have to get away before I drive myself crazy. Sitting around the house and thinking about his neighbour was rapidly becoming an obsession. *I need to do better,* he thought. *I should go out bar-hopping. Just pick some guy, take him to bed, and fuck him senseless. Or get fucked senseless.*

He enjoyed the park at any time of the year. The trails were decent for hiking even in the heart of winter, groomed just enough to walk, and there were no snowmobiles or heavy equipment permitted.

Walk far enough, he thought, *and you could imagine you were hundreds of clicks away from civilization.* He'd heard of people getting lost in the woods, though no one had ever died. *It's marked well enough that you will eventually find your way back onto a trail and to safety.*

Sean parked his car in the lot and got out. He chuckled softly. He came out to the park so often that he knew which spots were the best. Almost invariably, he parked in the exact same place every time.

He was wearing nylon windpants and a tee-shirt, along with comfortable sneakers. He adjusted his ball cap, shading his eyes. He thought about getting his jacket from the back seat, but decided he didn't need it. He did pick up his hiking belt and fasten it around his waist. The belt held a canteen and a few pouches for snacks and a few emergency supplies.

The park's office was lit up, but he ignored it. He'd seen the exhibits in there a dozen times before. He was more interested in getting out into the woods.

Should be private enough, he thought. There were only four cars in the lot, aside from his. *No one around today it seems.*

Adjusting the way his belt hung around his waist, he set off along one of his favourite trails.

The weather was perfect for hiking. The warm spring had come early this year, which certainly had been a welcome change from the cold and snow of the Canadian winter. When properly dressed, Sean enjoyed being outdoors in the winter as much as he did being outdoors at any other time of year, but he had to admit, it was a lot more pleasant to not have his teeth chattering while he walked.

It hadn't rained recently, so the ground was reasonably dry. While Sean did see some patches of mud on the trails, and the odd puddle still filling a rut or depression, almost all of the groomed trails and most of the rougher paths were clear and dry enough for him to enjoy with getting too muddy.

My sneakers will wash off anyway, he told himself. They'd been hosed down and left out on the porch to dry on more than one occasion. *Hell, they've been thrown into the washer and dryer a few times too.*

As he walked, he found that he was beginning to actually work up a bit of a sweat. Grinning, he peeled off his tee-shirt and enjoyed the feeling of the sun as it warmed the skin on his back and chest.

Sean turned off the main trail and started up one of the lesser trails. As he pushed his way through the junipers, he wondered if he'd made a mistake. *Maybe* this *wasn't actually meant to be a trail.* It could have just been a natural opening which looked like an almost overgrown trail...or it could be a path worn by deer or other animals.

I wonder if I should bring Jamie out here sometime. Just ask if he likes hiking and mention that I come out here all the time. He would be more than welcome to join me.

Sean stepped into a small clearing. He stopped and looked around.

The maples and pines were clustered thickly here, and the underbrush was equally lush. He couldn't see much of anything past the clearing.

Privacy.

I could bring him out here and wrestle him down onto the ground and have my way with him in the long grass. That thought was enough to make him start laughing again. *We'd probably get caught by the conservation officers or some passersby.* He'd read something in the paper last summer about a couple of guys getting busted for nocturnal activities in the park. *If they were stupid enough to fuck in the bathrooms, they deserved to get arrested for indecency.*

The noon-hour sun was hot against his bare skin. He pulled the small canteen of water away from his belt and took a drink. He'd flavoured the water with some drink crystals earlier and it tasted good.

Sitting down on the grass, Sean opened a pouch and snacked on a granola bar.

As he ate, he thought about some of the hikes he gone on in the past. He distinctly remembered this one time he'd gone with some high school buddies. They'd dared him to make the hike nude. Seeing as they four of them were in a remote area, he'd willingly stripped off everything except his hiking boots. The thrill of hiking in the nude had gotten his juices flowing.

I spent most of the hike with a hard-on, he recalled. His buddies had thought it was hilarious to see him walking and bouncing. *And they'd all stripped down before too long as well. Man, that was fun. The four of us walking and joking each other all naked.* They'd all gone skinny dipping on that trip too.

Returning to the present, Sean chuckled. *I wonder if I could get Jamie to go nude hiking with me?* He doubted it.

Sean realized that he had gotten a hard-on. The memories were that strong and still that arousing.

He lay back in the grass. His hand slipped past his waistband and into his boxers. He began to stroke himself. His eyes closed and he enjoyed the feel of the sun on chest and his hand on his cock.

He was really hard.

Then the roar of an engine broke his concentration.

"What the hell?" he asked, his eyes popping open. He sat up, frowning at the intrusion into the idyllic setting. "Is that a motorcycle?" He doubted it. There wouldn't be any such machines out here. He walked towards the sound. "I thought those damned things were banned from the conservation area," he said.

The machine and driver came into view. It wasn't a motorcycle, but an ATV.

From his clearing, Sean peered through the pine branches at the intruder.

It was a conservation officer.

The man slowed his four-wheeler to a stop and climbed off. He pushed his hat a bit further back on his head and looked around.

Sean wondered if the man could see him. He was still hard, his dick tenting out the front of his windpants.

The warden had short-cropped blond air and sunglasses covered his eyes. He swung his leg over the ATV as he climbed off. He flexed and stretched out his back, shoulders, and arms. His uniform shirt strained against his muscles.

Sean stared. The man must have stood a good six feet tall, and he filled his khaki-coloured uniform perfectly.

The warden stepped off the trail and into the bushes.

Sean flinched.

The warden hadn't apparently seen him. He walked vaguely in the direction Sean was standing in, but not directly. Instead, he stopped well short of the clearing, beside a particularly thick oak tree and unzipped the front of his pants and pulled out his dick.

A part of Sean's mind protested that he shouldn't be standing here and watching the warden taking a piss, but he couldn't look away. He was watching from a distance and the man didn't know he was there. *I could slip away if I wanted too,* he thought. He didn't move away.

The erection inside his own windpants and boxers was getting even harder.

Slowly, almost unconsciously, Sean slipped his hand back inside his waistband and started stroking himself again. He bit his lip to keep from groaning out loud.

The warden shook the last drops from his dick, then turned away from the oak.

To Sean's surprise, the man didn't put his dick back inside his pants.

He walked back to his ATV, his dick still hanging through his fly, and he leaned against the side of the black and red machine. He slowly caressed the base of his shaft.

"Come on out!" the conservation officer suddenly called. "I can see you."

Shit! Sean thought about turning and running.

"Come out here!"

Reluctantly, Sean stepped through the junipers. He tried to act nonchalant, tried to pretend that he wasn't shirtless and that the front of his nylon pants weren't tented almost obscenely.

A smile played across the man's square-jawed face. "I've seen you around before," he said in a deep voice. "You come here almost every week."

"I like the outdoors," Sean replied in a soft voice. He recognized the warden as well, though this was the closest he'd ever managed to get. *I'm gonna get banned,* he thought. *I'm gonna get arrested. I'm gonna—*

"I recognized your car in the lot." The conservation officer was smiling more broadly now. "I thought you'd come into the museum area today...I was really hoping you would." He was still stroking the base of his cock.

"I didn't mean to leave the trail," Sean protested. "I thought that was a smaller trail. I didn't mean to cross into forbidden territory."

The warden shrugged. "You haven't broken any laws," he said. "Like what you see?"

Sean realized that he was openly staring at the warden's crotch.

And the man's dick was growing larger.

"Do you like it or not?" Sean heard the conservation officer ask, and he could only nod his head dumbly.

"Good. I was hoping you'd say that." He gave his dick another stroke. "I've seen you in the parking lot and in the museum area checking out the visitors. Sneaking peaks at the other guys, not their girls. Watching theme bend over to get things from the car, staring at them as they point out birds in the marsh. Don't deny it."

Sean shook his head. He'd been caught flat-out.

"I've seen you checking me out too," the warden continued in that deep voice. "Staring at my ass and licking your lips. Looking at me while trying not to get caught."

"Yeah, it's true." Sean nodded his head.

"I've seen you undressing me with your eyes." He gave his hips a thrust to make his hard-on twitch. "Well...now you get to see the real thing in person."

Sean flinched.

"Get over here."

Sean obeyed. He could see the man's nametag on his right breast pocket. *Roy.*

"This machine is the ultimate vibrator," Roy announced. "Gets me rock hard every time I ride it."

Sean licked his lips nervously.

"Get down on your knees."

Sean did as he was told. The grass at the side of the trail was dry and soft. Roy's dick was right at eye level. It was stubby and thick, a drop of moisture at the end. *This isn't happening!* he thought. *We're in public! Anyone could walk up the trail and see us!*

"Get to it."

Sean opened his mouth and took the bulbous head into his mouth. Roy sighed.

Gradually, Sean took more of the shaft into his mouth. He took it slowly—Roy was thick—but eventually he managed to get it all in.

Roy was grunting, deep wordless noises that broadcast how much he was enjoying the blow-job.

Roy stood up to his full height, no longer slouching, and pushed down on Sean's shoulders.

Sean kept working at the thick cock in his mouth, sucking on it with all of the gusto he could muster.

Roy worked with him, thrusting his hips to shove his cock in and out of Sean's mouth. "Mmm, yeah," he grunted. "You suck like a pro. Yeah, take it all."

Sean gagged as the cock pushed too deep into his throat and Roy backed off slightly.

On his knees, Sean lost track of time. The dick in his mouth felt like it had been going in-and-out for hours, but it couldn't have been that long.

Roy pulled out of Sean's mouth and then pulled him to his feet. "Come over here." He dragged Sean closer to his ATV, and then bent him over the back.

Sean found his face resting on the seat of the ATV, his chest on the tarpaulin-covered cargo bay. He felt cool air gust over his ass as his windpants and boxers were abruptly yanked down.

"This should be fun...that's a nice ass you've got."

Sean could hear Roy fumbling with his uniform shirt and pants. He turned his head enough to look.

Roy had undone his uniform shirt, letting it hang open and expose the white tee-shirt underneath. He had also undone his belt and his pants were down around his knees.

"Are you—"

"Quiet."

Sean heard something tear—a condom wrapper?—and then he felt cool wetness dripping down the crack of his ass. A finger probed at his hole, loosening him. "Do it!" Sean hissed. He was harder now than ever, and he pushed his ass towards that probing finger.

Roy chuckled.

Sean jerked as Roy slapped his ass.

"Yeah, you've got a real nice ass." Roy rubbed his dick against Sean's ass cheeks.

"Do it...I'm yours."

Roy took a firm grip on Sean's shoulders. "Don't move." He moved his right hand down to his cock and pressed it against Sean's hole.

Sean gasped as he felt that thick cock push inside him.

Roy kept pressing, driving himself deeper and deeper. He had both hands on Sean's shoulders, holding the other man firmly against the ATV.

Sean was grunting loudly now, echoing Roy, as he was ridden. This warden was one amazing fuck!

Roy slowly pulled his cock almost all the way out, stopping with just the head still inside. Then he slammed his dick back in, as fast as he could manage. His grip on Sean's shoulders kept him from jerking away.

Sean could only grunt, like an animal, as Roy kept thrusting. His own dick was rock hard and pulsing upward towards his stomach, trapped between his stomach and the back of the ATV. The roughness of the tarpaulin was sensual against his cock-head and shaft and he knew that he wouldn't be able to hold himself for long.

Roy kept thrusting.

Sean could feel that all-too-familiar tightening in his crotch and he knew that he was about to cum. With a wild cry, he shot. Warm wetness spread across his stomach and chest.

That was all the encouragement Roy needed as he grunted even more loudly.

Sean was sure the other man was shooting his own load.

Roy froze.

Did he cum? Sean wondered if he'd be able to walk after this fuck session was over.

Roy pulled his cock out, then after a moment, he hauled Sean back to his own feet and spun him around so they were standing face-to-face.

Sean blinked, tiredly.

Roy pulled him forward and kissed him, deep and hard. His tongue probed deeply into Sean's mouth.

Sean returned the kiss, his hands reaching for Roy's waist and pulling the other man close. After the kiss finally ended, they continued to hold each other as their breathing slowly returned to normal.

Roy took a step back and stuffed his dick back into his briefs. He pulled his pants up and zipped. His uniform shirt was still hanging open and there was a wet stain on his tee-shirt. He looked down at it. "It'll dry before I get back," he said with a laugh. "Give me something to remember you by."

Sean blinked again.

Once we had composed ourselves, he stepped back and as he pulled his jeans and chaps back up, I saw that his t-shirt had a wet stain from a combination of his sweat and wiping the cum off my belly and chest. He noticed it too, and just laughed. "I think I'll enjoy sniffing this over the next few days. It'll be great to jerk off to the smell later."

Sean didn't reply.

"I'll be watching for you," Roy told him. "I know your car."

Sean nodded his head tiredly.

"You should stop by the office," he said. "We've got a nice comfortable couch in there. The door is thick enough to stifle any sound. It has a lock too."

"I'll keep that in mind," Sean replied.

"Good, now put some clothes on before I arrest you for indecent exposure." Roy smiled and waved. He started the ignition.

As the ATV roared off along the trail, Sean pulled his boxers and pants back up. Then he stumbled stiffly back to the clearing to find his tee-shirt.

"Fuck me," he mumbled. He pulled the canteen from his belt and drained it.

Chapter Eight

"You don't stay home on many weekends, do you mate?" Jamie commented as he watched Sean unloading his fishing gear from the trunk of his car.

"No, I like to take advantage of having a couple of days off from work to go fishing. Get away from the city and travel a bit. Sometimes I load up my backpack and go hiking through one of the parks. Or the conservation area."

"You're a real outdoorsman then?"

"Yeah, I like to think that I am." Sean glanced at Jamie.

Jamie's tee-shirt and jeans were still dusty and dirty from his day's work. He was grubby, but it made him look more rugged and sexy.

I couldn't see him wearing a suit, Sean thought. *But I bet he cleans up really nicely when he has too.* He certainly had the build of a construction worker.

"I think I spent more time growing up under the open sky than under a roof," Jamie commented. "I was outside all the time. Tanned darker than an Abbo."

"I've always enjoyed the outdoors. I must have walked hundreds of klicks through the Little Cataraqui Conservation Area. And up around Desert Lake is some really nice scenery. Small stunted pine trees literally clinging to the cliffs above the rippling water. Loons calling. Ducks splashing as they land. Floating in the middle of it all, waiting for the fish to bite."

"Sounds like a great way to spend a weekend."

"It is. I like the solitude—being able to get away is a welcome relief from my office job." Sean paused, taking a close look at Jamie. "Do you ever fish?"

Jamie looked back at him, and then he nodded. He was standing with his hands stuffed in the pockets of his jeans. "I've gone out to sea a few times back home. Never tackled any of your local fish though."

"We don't have marlins or sharks or whatever," Sean told him with a grin, "but we do have some nice trout or bass. Might even find the odd salmon, if you hit the right river."

Jamie nodded his head. He reached up to push his ball cap further back on his head.

"Would you like to come with me?" Sean asked.

"Fishing?"

"Yeah...come for the weekend."

"You sure?"

"Of course." Sean was rapidly falling deeper in love with the idea of getting his hunky neighbour alone in the woods. "We'll have a great time."

Jamie followed him out of the garage.

Sean hit the remote and the door began to close. It was almost soundless and it rolled smoothly down its track.

"You got it fixed up?" Jamie asked.

"Yeah, I finally remembered to call Eastern about it." *They were the ones who installed it, they might as well be the ones to fix it.* "I guess they sent someone around on the weekend to do the work." *I wonder if he was cute.* No way to tell now.

Jamie was nodding his head. "Seem to have done an okay job."

"Yeah, they're pretty reliable. Jacob hires them too."

"Nothing wrong with his garage door."

"No reason there should be. He has it serviced every year...I'm just not that picky." Sean shrugged. "About the garage door at least. I do take care of my fishing gear."

"I saw that. I'm like you, I think. I like to use something until it wears out."

I'd like to use you until you wear out, Sean thought. *I wonder how long your batteries will last?* He gave himself a shake. "Any word from Jacob?"

"He might around on the weekend. Might not. Apparently the lottery winners are having some issues with the designs. The coach house slash guest-house is too close to the main house. Or something."

"Oh."

"Yeah, I was chatting with him on the phone the other night. He's ready to come back home and tell them to call him when they make up their minds."

"I can't say that I blame him for feeling like that."

Jamie shrugged. "I prefer my job to his. Go to the work-site, do my job, come home at the end of the day. Hot shower, good meal, a few drinks, and then find a mate for a quick shag if I'm lucky."

"Have you been that...er, *lucky*?"

At that question, Jamie chuckled. "Once or twice, mate."

"Oh, good for you."

Jamie was still chuckling.

Sean bit his lip.

* * *

"*Already* making plans for another weekend away?" Jackie was shaking her head as she stood in the office doorway. "I really don't see the appeal in camping. I never have."

"I enjoy it." Sean stood up and walked away from his desk.

"All alone in a tent in the woods? One of these days you're going to get attacked by a bear."

Oh, I can always hope, Sean thought as he walked towards the break room. He'd met a few *bears* online and Karl, one of his first lovers, had been a very good teacher.

Jackie was following down the carpeted hallway after him, still rambling on about the numerous and varied dangers of being out in the woods alone. There was the risk of the boat sinking, or Sean drowning, or simply having a seizure in the night. "And who would ever know?" she asked. "Who would know to alert the authorities?"

"Who would know if anything like that happened to me at home?" Sean countered. "I sleep alone, you know."

"Oh."

Sean continued walking.

"But you're in the woods. It's more dangerous out there."

"Is it?"

"Of course...you're out in the *woods*." Jackie shook her head at his foolishness. "It's the wilderness, isn't it? Animals and things. Lots of dangers. Bears. Wolves. Snakes."

"I guess it does sound dangerous." Sean chuckled. *I've never seen a bear out there, or a wolf.* "Anyway, I won't be alone this time."

"Oh?" She looked surprised at his words. Her eyes narrowed suddenly. "I thought you always went off on these things alone."

"I've got a friend going this time."

"Anyone I know?" she asked. She actually leaned closer to him, as if to hear him more clearly.

"No...just taking one of my neighbours along."

"Oh."

"No one you know." Sean stopped in front of the men's room door. "We're going to spend the weekend fishing and living rough."

"I bet Jackie likes it rough," a deep voice commented.

Sean turned his head even as Jackie sniffed loudly. "Hello, Kevin." He gave Kevin another look as the security guard followed him into the lavatory.

Kevin Day was definitely worth a second and even a fifth look. He kept his brown hair cut into a regulation crew-cut and the black shirt and pants of his security uniform moulded themselves to his body.

Sean tried not to stare. He had gotten a hard-on the very first time he had walked past the security guard at the front desk. After two years, he still enjoyed arriving at the office in the morning and greeting the man. *So what does your* weapon *look like?*

Unfortunately for him, Kevin did not walk towards the urinals and unzip himself. He moved instead to stand in the front of the sink, standing there and washing his hands. "So you're heading off into the wilderness yet again?"

"Yeah. Going away for the weekend."

"Sounds like fun."

Sean finished and zipped his slacks back up. "It is fun," he said. "You should try it sometime."

"Not enough beer in town to get me out there."

"One of these days, I'll take that as a personal challenge," Sean told him as he washed his own hands at the sink.

"So you want to get me out way out in the woods. Get me drunk and then you'll drag me into the tent and have your way with me?" Kevin asked him, a grin playing across his face. "Or are you just hoping to talk me into just going skinny dipping?"

"How many beers will it take to get you skinny dipping?"

Kevin shook his head. "Not too many."

Oh really? Sean's eyes widened and he reached for the paper towel dispenser.

"Later." Kevin walked out through the door.

Sean frowned as the door swung closed. *What the hell was that about?* Was Kevin coming onto him? *Not that I would turn him down, of course, not a chance of that. But I thought he had a girlfriend.*

* * *

Sean walked past the steam room without bothering to look inside. He had been coming to this fitness centre for months, but the though of just sitting and baking in the sauna didn't appeal to him. He liked the pool.

God, I've always loved the pool he thought. *Surrounded by hunky men in skimpy swimsuits and nothing else.* It was so easy to get a nice long look at a man's nylon-covered crotch without him even noticing...and the water helped hide the inevitable hard-on.

Until it's time to get out of the pool, of course. Then he just had to relax, think of other things, and wait until the erection went limp.

Now he was on his way to enjoy a hot shower before the drive home. Rush-hour traffic would be over and done—which was the main reason he chose to work out after work.

It was also raining today. It had been pouring since before noon, with thunder and lots of lightning, so he knew that he would be cooped up in the house all night. *At least I can go for a swim in here*, he thought.

Standing naked under the shower, he let the hot water cascade over his arms and chest. His muscles were still aching from all the laps he had swum.

He was just starting to soap up his cock and balls—and giving himself a pretty good hard-on in the process—when he heard someone whistling and entering the shower area.

He quickly turned around and faced the wall.

"How's the water?"

Sean glanced over his shoulder to see a former co-worker's face.

Andrew Musgrave was looking at him.

Sean stared back. "Drew!" he exclaimed. His gaze dropped down to the other man's crotch before he could catch himself. "How are you?" He could feel his cheeks growing hot.

"They're good." Andrew was smiling. He was quite openly checking out Sean's wet and naked body. His eyes lingered, for just a moment, on Sean's groin and the erection he had. "I haven't seen you around here."

"I—er...."

"I saw you down in the pool earlier, but I wanted to spend some time on the treadmill. I'm trying to get in shape."

"You look fine to me," Sean told him honestly. His dick was getting harder and he desperately tried to will his erection away.

"I want to run in the county marathon this year. I'm still building up my stamina." Andrew reached for the shower taps and turned on the water. He looked back at Sean, an amused smiling playing across his mouth. "Other than that, I'm still working hard."

"Your folks are doing okay?"

"The store is busier than they ever thought. Which is why I'm so busy."

Sean turned towards him. By now his hard-on had mostly gone away.

Andrew was standing there, his face under the shower spray. As the water caressed its way down his body, over his muscular chest and flat stomach, he looked like a statue that had been carved out of stone and left in someone's garden in the rain.

Sean tried to make himself look away—but as Andrew moved under the spray, he could see the other man's flaccid cock hanging down and it looked huge! Sean quickly looked back towards the other man's face.

Andrew was smiling openly now.

Busted! Sean thought. *Damn.*

"It looks like you've been working out," Andrew commented as he worked the soapy washcloth across his chest. "I don't recall you looking that lean when I last saw you."

"Well..." Sean's voice trailed off. He had a sudden warm feeling inside the pit of his stomach and his dick twitched.

"Lots of those nature hikes and camping trips you were always talking about, I bet. The healthy lifestyle seems to be working for you." He paused, still wearing a somewhat quizzical little smile. "I know this sounds like an odd request, but would you mind soaping up my back and shoulders for me? I'm a bit stiff right now and I can't quite reach."

Sean's mouth went dry, but he quickly nodded his head. "Sure."

"Thanks, man. I owe you one." He leaned against the tiles of the shower wall, spreading his legs so that Sean could move stand in-between them and reach all of his back.

I can't believe this is happening! Sean thought. Working up a good lather, he started to soap Andrew's shoulders, working my way to his spine. "You said that you feel stiff? You probably could use a massage."

"Yeah, that would be nice."

Sean adjusted his stance, then began kneading Andrew's back with his hands. "How's that feel?"

Andrew just moaned softly.

Sean worked his way lower, feeling the other man's muscles under his fingers.

Andrew's ass-cheeks quivered as Sean approached his waist. "Mmm, that's really good," he moaned. "Feel free to carry on."

I was hoping you'd say that. Almost as strongly as he was hoping that no one else would walk into the showers. Sean's cock was rock-hard by now, and he added a third hope to his list. *Don't turn around*! He kept massaging Andrew's back.

Andrew reached out and caught Sean's hand. "Don't forget these muscles...they've been working hard." He moved Sean's hand down lower.

Sean was groping Andrew's ass. *It's as firm as it looked under his slacks every day.* Squirting more body-wash gel into his hands, he began to knead both of those firm muscular globes. His dick was throbbing with the urge to stroke himself.

Andrew moaned.

Sean slid his fingers down his ass-crack, separating his cheeks, and then slipped his fingers a bit further down to tease the edge of his hole.

"Fuck, Sean, just keep doing what you're doing."

By now, Sean was too far gone to even think about stopping—no matter who might suddenly walk in on them. He slipped a finger up

Andrew's ass as his other hand went down under his spread legs to hold his balls.

The sharp intake of breath betrayed Andrew's excitement.

Sean glanced down—his hard dick was almost touching those tight ass-cheeks.

When Andrew suddenly reached back and grabbed his throbbing cock, Sean felt a momentary surge of panic.

Andrew began to stroke his shaft.

Now it was Sean who tried not to moan too loudly.

"Shove it in me!" Andrew pleaded. "Don't stop now."

Sean was standing there, the head of his cock resting against Andrew's hole. "I don't have anything with me," he muttered.

"Are you clean?" Andrew asked.

"Yeah."

"Then fuck me." He pushed his ass back and Sean felt his soaped-up dick slid along the crack.

Sean grabbed at his waist to catch his balance.

"Fuck me!" Andrew pleaded.

Sean was stunned at how quickly this had happened, but his cock was loving every second. He tried to move, to get a better stance, and line up his dick with Andrew's hole, but the soapy friction was too much and he exploded with a startled gasp.

"Fuck, that was quick." Andrew sounded amused. He turned around, so that the shower could rinse his back. "It's my turn now!"

Sean stumbled, still trying to catch his breath after cumming. His eyes widened as the other man turned. Andrew's cock was huge. Thick and long. "Holy shit!" The idle chatter from the office had no idea just how massive he was!

"My turn," Andrew repeated.

"There is no fucking way you are shoving that inside me!" Sean protested. "Not here." And not without a lot of lube and some extensive foreplay!

Andrew just smiled and used his hands to guide Sean down onto his knees.

Sean stared at the cock which was slapping against his cheeks.

"We don't have time to really play...and this is hardly the place." Andrew shifted position so that his dick pressed against Sean's mouth. "So we'll just make it quick."

Sean opened his mouth as wide as he could. The feel of the other man's dick in his mouth was overwhelming. *And I thought Roy was big*! There was no way that entire dick was going to fit inside his mouth.

But Andrew was determined to try.

Sean gagged as he was overwhelmed. He actually wondered if he was going to pass out from a lack of oxygen.

"Yeah, take it!" Andrew gasped. "Fuck, yeah!"

Sean winced as the other man tried to push his dick even deeper into his mouth.

Then the cock pulsed and his mouth was flooded with cum. He tried to swallow all of it, but there was just too much, too quickly, and it spilled out of his lips and down his chin.

Andrew reached down to stroke his shaft, encouraging every last drop to come out.

Sean felt somewhat light-headed as Andrew finally pulled out. He swallowed what he could, and let the shower water rinse the rest from his mouth.

"Wow, I had no idea that you were such a good little cock-sucker," Andrew commented as he soaped up his softening dick and rinsed. "The rumour around the office was that you were gay, but no one ever confirmed it."

Sean blinked, still dazed.

Andrew pulled him to his feet and washed off his face. "You were great."

Sean opened his mouth to say something, but he shut it just as quickly when two more naked men in walked into the shower room.

Both were older, white-haired, with flabby, hairy bodies. They were chattering away in Italian to one another as they walked towards the unused showerheads.

Sean averted his eyes.

Andrew finished his shower and left the shower room.

Chapter Nine

Sean clicked off the television. There was nothing good on; even with all the cable options, there was nothing worth watching. He leaned back in his rocking chair and stared through the window. It was still raining.

Two days of rain...this pretty much sucks. He was praying for good weather on the weekend. *I don't want us to be rained out.*

Of course, if it did pour rain while they were camping, then he and Jamie would most likely be confined to the tent. *I might have a shot at him then.* Sean laughed to himself. *And he'd probably punch my lights out.* He sighed softly and reached for his after-work drink.

Jamie's *Mazda* pulled into the driveway.

Sean leaned forward in his chair. He thought about getting up and calling Jamie to come in and visit for a bit.

Jamie stepped away from his car. He was still dressed in his grubby construction gear, his rain-soaked tee-shirt plastered to his chest. The knees of his jeans were muddy.

A second car pulled up and a man got out.

Sean froze, his hand resting on the doorknob of his front door.

The second man was older, wearing a blue shirt and jeans. He looked grubby, his clothes as dirty as Jamie's. They talked for a moment, and then he followed Jamie around to the backyard.

Sean's eyes narrowed.

* * *

Sean walked through the grocery store, a blue plastic basket hanging in his hand. The meat bunkers were being refilled so he decided to grab a few other things while waiting for the steaks to come out from the back.

"...so I've told my dad that we're getting married."

Sean smiled as he head the deep voice from around the corner. It belonged to the cutest clerk at the store.

Stan.

Dodging around two senior citizens, Sean stopped and pretended to look at the bread racks. In truth, he kept darting glances at the clerk.

Stan—thank God for staff name tags—had short blond hair. His arms had a light dusting of hair, and he filled out his green polo shirt and black jeans quite nicely. His body looked muscular, but not overly built.

Fuck, he's hot. Sean shopped at this store just for the scenery.

Stan and another guy—much less hot with his stringy hair, patchy goatee, and sickly-pale skin—were restocking one of the centre aisle displays with bags of pasta from boxes on a cart.

Sean looked back at the bread. *I should get some buns for tonight...and I bet Stan's buns would be really nice to squeeze. His buns with a little whipped cream and I could have quite the desert.*

"Can I help you?"

Sean flinched. "Oh...uh." He was staring into Stan's face.

The clerk had an amused smile, as if he was used to finding customers being distracted by something on the shelves.

I bet he is use to it...I bet every gay man in the city shops here just to see him. Sean licked his lips. "I'm just waiting for the fresh steaks."

"They should be coming out shortly. You want me to check for you?"

"Yes, thank you."

Stan nodded. "T-bone?" he asked. "What kind were you waiting for?"

"T-bone is good...something for grilling later. I've got company coming over later for a barbeque."

"Something with a bone is always best for that," Stan agreed. "I'll be right back." He walked towards the backroom.

Sean watched him. *He has a very nice ass.* For a moment, Sean wished he could be reincarnated as a pair of black *Wranglers.*

The other clerk had vanished with the cart.

Sean picked up a package of Kaiser buns. *I wonder if Jamie likes Kaisers? Maybe I should get something else?* He decided to keep the Kaisers.

Stan emerged from the backroom. "I've got a nice piece of meat for you," he said.

"Sorry?" Sean gave his head a shake.

"I said I've got a nice piece of meat." Stan was smiling. He had dimples, which made him look young and boyish. "Something with a good-sized bone in it."

Sean realized that Stan was carrying a package of steaks.

"Here you go. I hope they're what you wanted. If not," he added, "I can go find you some other hunk of beef."

Down boy! Sean told his hardening dick. *He's just tormenting me.* Sean wondered if Stan had ever been jumped by a male customer before. "They look perfect." He took the package in his hands. "Thank you."

"Anytime," Stan told him. "If you don't see what you want, just ask." With another grin, he walked away.

Sean stared after him. *I want you naked in my bed,* he thought. *God, I've become a lecherous slut.* His neighbour, the conservation warden, Andrew, and now Stan. Though he'd been lusting after Stan for quite some time now. *I need a long vacation.*

"Those look like nice cuts. Nice and meaty."

Sean turned around at the familiar voice. "Hi, Jamie."

Jamie gave him a friendly smile. "Fancy meeting you here."

"Small world."

"Yep. You man enough to eat four steaks?"

"I'd like to say *yes*, but not usually at one time. Actually, I was hoping you'd be free this Thursday night for dinner. I was thinking we could finish making our plans for the camping trip then."

"That, mate, depends on how you're cooking those things."

"Barbeque."

"Ah, the only way." Jamie chuckled, and then nodded his head. "In that case, yes I'm free to join you. Should I bring anything with me?"

"Just your appetite. Oh, bring a salad, if you want. I've got buns and meat so we're good otherwise."

"All right. See you tomorrow night then."

Sean nodded. "Bye." He watched Jamie saunter across the store. *Who was your friend the other night?* He wanted to shout that question out, but he bit his tongue. *Co-worker or drinking buddy,* he told himself. *None of your business anyway. Christ, Sean, you've been jerking off multiple times a day and you jumped Andrew the other day...what more do you want?*

He wanted Jamie.

* * *

The smoke from the barbeque carried the scent of sizzling beef.

It smells amazing. Sean licked his lips. He could barely wait for supper.

"Nothing like a nice thick steak done on a barbie."

"Yep." Sean nodded at Jamie. "Especially when they've been cooked just right."

"Right you are, mate. Sometimes you just want to have the whole bloody cow walk past so you can rip off what you want." Jamie chuckled and leaned back even further in the chair.

Sean checked on the steaks. *Almost done,* he thought, noting the grill lines. He glanced back at his guest.

Jamie had his legs spread apart, lounging comfortably in the chair, and his baggy shorts were hanging open.

If I stoop down, I might be able to get a peak. I could pretend to be tying my shoe. Sean gave himself a quick mental shake. *Stop thinking like that. You can't jump the cute neighbour...however much you want too.* He looked back at the steaks. *Anyway, you're not wearing shoes.*

Jamie took a long drink out of his beer.

"So how does it compare?" Sean asked him.

"Pardon?"

"How does the beer compare?"

"Better than what the Yanks drink. That piss is like drinking water."

Sean chuckled. "Most of us think so too."

"I mean, given the taste of it...why bother?"

"You should try the non-alcoholic version."

Jamie snorted. "How're the steaks?"

"Probably done."

"Good. I'm starving."

"Hand me a plate and I'll serve."

Sean took another bite from the salad. Jamie's coleslaw vinaigrette was amazing.

"Old family recipe," Jamie had said when he brought the bowl over. *"I think you'll like it. Everyone does."*

Sean took another bite. "You were right. This salad is amazing. I'd marry you to get the recipe." Then he realized what he had just said and almost bit his tongue. "I mean, you said it was a family recipe so—"

Jamie laughed.

Sean hid his face behind his beer.

Jamie had already eaten half his steak. "We still on for the weekend?"

"Yeah, I hope so." Sean nodded his head. "You having second thoughts?"

"No, but I wasn't sure you meant your invitation."

"Why wouldn't I?"

"Some people say things in polite conversation. They don't mean them though."

"Jamie, I would never say anything to you that I didn't mean." Sean blinked as the words registered. "I..." He hastily took another drink from the bottle in his hand.

Jamie had a faint smile playing across his face.

"Would you prefer a cabin or are you okay with just sleeping in a tent?"

"I've slept rough before." Jamie rubbed at his eyes. "Plenty of times. Even done it with just a sleeping bag under the stars."

"I usually just use a tent for overnight trips—too many mosquitoes and deerflies otherwise. You'd wake up eaten half alive. I do know a friend who has a cabin I can usually borrow if you'd prefer that."

"You're the guy in charge...we'll do whatever you want too."

Sean gave him a smile. "You'll love it. We'll have a blast."

Chapter Ten

Sean turned off the highway and onto the dirt road. The gravel crunched under his tires. "It's not far now," he told Jamie.

"I've been enjoying the drive. The scenery is so different from back home."

"No barren outback here." The pine trees were thick along the road. "Plenty of wildlife. Lots of birds—loons especially—some deer, the odd moose. Might see a bear, but that's really rare." He had only ever seen one bear in seven years. "You should be able to get a glimpse of the lake from the road any moment now."

"The outback isn't as desolate as you lot think it is. There's plenty of life...most of it poisonous."

"You won't find as much of that around here," Sean told him. "Just let me point out the poison ivy and you should be fine."

The car rounded a curve, climbed up a bit of a slope, and the trees gave way to a vista of the lake.

It was sparkling in the sunlight, smooth as glass.

"Wow."

Sean smiled, hearing the wonder in Jamie's voice. *He sounds like I did the first time I saw the lake.*

Sean drove the car into the grassy field, pulling it well clear of the road before he killed the motor and climbed out.

Jamie followed him out, standing stiff for a few moments, before stretching out his arms and legs.

Sean looked around. The tranquility of the park was a complete change from the city. He inhaled deeply...the pines were strong. "This is a good spot to park."

"Is it?" Jamie asked him.

"Oh yeah. I've had some great times here." Sean gestured. "We just have to follow that stream for about half a kilometre or so and we'll be at the lake. The cove there is perfect for camping. I've been coming here for years...." *Ever since that first time...*

Sean looked around the clearing with a satisfied nod of his head. Sylvester has been right, this really was the perfect spot to pitch a tent. The pine trees rose up, easily twenty metres or more, and a narrow stream was gurgling softly, in counter point to the birds chirping in the trees.

The July sun was hot and Sean wiped sweat from his forehead. The long hike through the forest had been tiring, and setting up the tent had felt like it had taken longer than normal. He was sure that was just the heat making it seem that way.

The heat really was wearying.

Sean tossed his pack inside the tent, then straightened back up. He quickly crossed the clearing.

The stream was flowing swiftly.

Sean walked towards it. He could hear it calling to him, like a mythical Siren. No real thinking was required—the cool water would be a fabulous way to recover from the long hike.

No one else was around. Other than a handful of people hiking the trail, Sean hadn't seen anyone else in hours. And the trail itself was dozens of metres away now, screened by a thick copse of pine trees.

If you didn't know this clearing was here, you'd never find it. Sean chuckled to himself. *Good thing too.* Privacy would be appreciated. *Nothing is worse than trying to sleep in your tent and having to listen to college kids partying right next to you.* When he went camping, he left technology behind so that he could be alone.

Privacy is good for something else too, he thought as he eyed the stream. He hastily kicked off his sneakers and pulled off his socks. He lifted his green tee-shirt over his head and then unbuckled his khaki hiking shorts. He stepped out of them.

A gust of warm breeze brushed across his chest and legs.

"Fuck it, I'm going skinny dipping." Sean yanked down his boxer-briefs and dropped them on top of his other clothing.

The cool water felt really refreshing around his body. He sank down into it, enjoying the sensations. The streambed, at least in this stretch, was mostly smooth rocks. It wasn't deep enough to swim in, but it was just deep enough to submerge himself.

Eventually, Sean waded out of the knee-deep stream. He didn't feel like going fishing, so he decided to sprawl out on the grassy bank and work on his tan.

He lazed alongside the stream for a good half hour, letting the sun play across his naked body. Unconsciously, his hand slowly wandered down to begin stroking his semi-hard cock. He worked himself to his full eight inches thinking about a pair of hunky hikers whom he had seen on the trail.

A branched snapped loudly, breaking him out of his daydreams.

Sean quickly scrambled back to his feet, looking about for a branch or a rock to use in defending himself against the onslaught of a beer or moose.

A tall male figure emerged from the trees.

Sean exhaled in relief at the figure being a man.

Then he remembered that he was stark naked and sporting a hard-on.

For one brief moment, Sean thought that the man was wearing a conservation officer's uniform. The khaki shirt and olive green shorts certainly resembled a uniform, and they were clinging snugly to his muscular body. There was a definite bulge in the front of his shorts.

The man didn't say a word either. He was simply stood there, openly studying Sean's naked body.

Sean could feel his face burning. He knew that he was blushing at being caught while jerking off. Despite his embarrassment, though, he couldn't help but notice what a handsome face the other man had. His almost-uniform only helped accentuate a body built for survival anywhere, not just the woods. As Sean stared back, his still-hard cock twitched.

A faint smile twisted the man's face.

Shit. Sean glanced towards the pile of clothing he had tossed aside so cavalierly half an hour earlier. "Uh, sorry about this."

"It's not a problem." The other man was now smiling. He didn't look angry or offended. "It ain't nothing I haven't seen before." He walked across the clearing, coming closer to the gurgling stream. "I'm just out hiking...thought I might come and soak my feet in the stream for a bit."

"Oh." Sean took a step towards his clothes. "Let me just grab—"

"Don't bother on my account." The man was still grinning. "I'm just enjoying the view."

Sean felt his face grow ever hotter.

"Just wish I had my camera with me." He grimaced. "Figures, the one time I leave it in the jeep." He glanced towards Sean's tent.

"I don't have one either." Sean managed a shrug, striving to be nonchalant as he felt his blush finally fading. "I like to get away from civilization when I go camping."

"I can see that."

Sean felt himself blushing again.

The man removed his hat and ran his fingers through his crew-cut blond hair. "Name's Colin."

Sean's cock jumped again.

The man continued walking across the grass. When he got close to where Sean stood, he bent down and picked up his discarded boxer-briefs. He didn't hand them over immediately, either, but lifted them to his nose and inhaled.

Sean licked his lips. He could see the bulge in front of Colin's shorts growing larger.

Colin noticed where Sean's gaze had gone. "I was enjoying watching you play with yourself," he said. "I didn't want to interrupt you, least not before the show was over, but just going at it alone is a waste." He reached out and ran his fingers lightly down Sean's chest, across his stomach, and then ended by gripping his cock. "A real waste."

Sean wasn't sure what to say as Colin began to stroke his hard-on. He simply moaned softly.

Grinning, Colin unbuttoned his short-sleeved shirt, slowly with only one hand, and exposed a tanned and hairy chest. Then he reached down to unfasten his shorts.

Sean reached for them first. He pulled the zipper down and popped the button, allowing the shorts to drop to the ground.

Sean stared at the man's cock as it sprang to attention. *No underwear,* one part of his mind noted. It looked to be a match for his own eight inches but it was a lot thicker. "Speaking of nice views...." He was getting so excited by this completely unexpected encounter, that he almost blew his load right then and there.

Colin gently pushed Sean down into the soft grass. "You're all mine, buddy." He climbed on top of Sean and began running his hands all over the other man's body.

Sean groaned with pleasure.

Beads of sweat dripped from Colin's broad chest. His dark brown nipples were erect and stood out like little raisins.

Sean reached up and pinched them as Colin's hands worked themselves toward his cock.

"Fuck yeah!" Colin gasped. His own hands were focussed on stroking and massaging Sean's cock.

Sean just couldn't hold back—it was too much for him—and he cried out as he came. Thick white cum erupted out of his throbbing dick and splattered across his chest.

Colin was wearing a wide smile.

"Damn...that was fast." Sean was still panting for breath.

Colin just continued to smile. He used his fingers to wipe the cream off Sean's belly and then teasingly licked it off.

Sean managed a weak grin. "I should have more stamina. I'm not some over-horny sixteen year old."

"You sure about that?" Colin asked, with a chuckle. "So, how about some help?" Laying down on his back, he wrapped his fingers around his own hard-on and started to stroke it. "Pinch my nipples."

"Sure." Sean reached for them. He grabbed the hard nubs in his fingers and gave them a twist.

"Harder!" Colin growled. "Pinch them harder!"

Sean obeyed and the man's moans echoed through the clearing.

Colin continued stroking himself, rubbing his body and legs against Sean's. Drops of pre-cum were oozing out of his dick.

Sean grunted in surprise as his flaccid dick began to grow hard again. He looked down at himself, startled by how quickly he was ready for a second round. *What the fuck?* The joint sensations of their rubbing bodies, along with the sight of the blond, tanned stranger jerking himself, was too just too arousing a sight.

Abruptly, Colin rolled over and onto Sean's body. His leaking cock brushed Sean's stomach and then his chest, until it hung in front of his face.

Tentatively, Sean gently licked his tongue along the tip.

"Fuck yeah!" Colin grunted. "Put some effort into it!" He rubbed his throbbing hard-on across Sean's nose and chin. His balls bounced against Sean's neck.

"I want to taste you so badly." Sean opened his mouth wide. He swallowed the entire head.

Colin rose onto his haunches and started to thrust his hips forward, pushing his cock deeper into Sean's eager mouth.

The back of Sean's throat relaxed despite Colin' almost-desperate thrusting into his mouth. The heat and fury of his coming climax was evident. Sweat clouded Sean's vision as the man's washboard stomach heaved above him.

With a loud yell, Colin let go and the cream within his balls filled Sean's mouth.

That was all it took for Sean to lose control, and cum gushed forth from his dick for the second time.

Colin collapsed to the ground beside Sean and both men lay in the grass gasping for breath.

"I must have hiked along the trails for hours the first time I came here," Sean explained. He tried to ignore the hard-on which had popped up during his stroll down memory lane. *Maybe Jamie won't see it.* "I'd left my car up closer to the highway. Sylvester didn't tell me about this convenient parking spot being right here."

"I don't mind a bit of a hike." Jamie stretched out his arms, trying to work out the last kinks from the ride. "I might try going on one later."

"You won't get lost, will you?"

"I hope not." He grinned. "Just have to hope I don't get attacked by any bears." He winked at Sean.

Sean just stared back at him.

* * *

The fire crackled in the small rock-encircled fire pit.

A loon cried out.

Sean gave a start as Jamie shifted positions and ended up leaning against him.

"This is nice," Jamie said.

Is it ever, Sean thought. "Yeah, it is nice," he said aloud.

Another loon called.

An owl hooted.

"Are those bats?" Jamie asked.

Sean looked. "Yeah. Catching insects. Not bloodsuckers out here."

"Just a few too many of these bloody mosquitoes."

"Yeah, always mosquitoes." Sean chuckled. "I guess we should think about getting ready for bed."

"Yeah." Jamie headed towards the tent.

Sean started to follow after him. *This should be good,* he thought. *Damn.* He turned and headed into the forest a little bit. He pulled out his dick and took a leak.

Sean hurried to the tent.

Jamie was already inside, with only his tee-shirt removed so far.

Good, I didn't miss very much of the show, Sean thought. He kicked off his sandals, and then started to pull his own tee-shirt over his head. He chuckled. Stripping off their clothes inside a tent required considerable effort—both men were trying to undress at the same time, without enough space for either to stand fully erect or move around without bumping into each other. "Do you want me to wait outside?" Sean finally asked. *Or do you mind me watching you strip?*

"No, I'm not shy." Jamie was unzipping his jeans now. Bending over, he pushed them down his legs.

Sean stared at Jamie's ass. The tight red briefs hugged two firm butt-cheeks and he had to physically fight the urge to yank the cotton down. He also couldn't help but stare at the other man's body.

Jamie's body lived up to every single one of Sean's fantasies. He was slender, in good shape, with a good covering of hair on his tanned body.

Where are your tan lines? Sean wondered. He thought he could just make out the outline of Jamie's cock and balls through the cotton as Jamie turned. Sean quickly looked away, hoping his staring hadn't been noticed.

Sean finished taking his own pants off and was thankful that his boxer shorts were more covering than briefs. *I should keep the tee-shirt on,* he thought. His dick was half-erect and getting harder.

Jamie didn't seem to notice anything out of the ordinary. He climbed into his sleeping bag and laid his head on the inflatable pillow. "This is surprisingly comfortable."

"Yeah, they are." Sean quickly finished stripping and climbed into his own sleeping bag. *Yeah, he didn't notice my hard-on.* He lay on his side. *I wish I could take proper care of it.* He was able to stroke himself, carefully, but he knew he couldn't have a proper jerk-off session with the other man so close. *He'd notice that!*

Jamie turned off the light.

Sean sighed. *Now to try and sleep with him right there.* Sleep would not come quickly, he suspected. Not with Jamie laying so close. He hear could Jamie's steady breathing.

Chapter Eleven

The lake was placid. A few cloud could be seen on the horizon.

Sean was half-drowsing in the back of the small inflatable boat. He had dressed in a pair of jeans and a short-sleeved shirt. He'd also warned Jamie to dress similarly. *The sunlight reflecting off the water could cause some serious sunburns if we aren't careful. There will be no fun in spending the weekend burned as red as a lobster.* He eyed Jamie from under the brim of his hat.

Jamie was wearing a tee-shirt and faded jeans. The other man was seating in the front of the boat, and not paying much attention to his fishing rod. He'd been surprised when Sean had dragged the small case out of the car and hooked the motorized pump to the car battery to inflate the boat.

'Did you think we were going to fish from shore?' Sean had asked

'Well, I didn't see a boat trailer when we came up,' Jamie had replied. 'I had thought we might be borrowing or renting one.'

'No place around here to do that. This lake is much too isolated.'

'How isolated?'

'No cottages, no real campgrounds. If we're lucky, there won't be another living soul for twenty or thirty kilometres.'

'Bloody hell, mate. I never thought of us being so isolated.'

'Like being back in the outback?'

"Sort of.'

A gull swooped low over their heads, then wheeled about and flew back towards the shore.

If Jamie did get sunburned, Sean thought, *then I'd have the perfect excuse to strip him down and rub ointment all over him. Strip him naked...rub and stroke his arms and legs...work my way across his taunt body.*

Sean gave himself a shake. *Down boy.* The crotch of his jeans was tented from his growing hard-on. *Damn.* He shifted positions, trying to ease the strain his cock was feeling inside the jeans.

Jamie never seemed to notice.

The bank of black clouds were growing darker and getting a lot closer.

"The wind's picking up."

Sean nodded. "Yeah, we really should head back to shore." He tried to calculate how fast the clouds were moving. "We don't want to be caught out here if a storm hits."

"Looks like it's gonna be a bad one." Jamie pulled the brim of his ball cap a bit lower as the wind gusted around them.

Sean pulled at the motor cord.

It spluttered, but didn't catch.

"Oh come on, you stupid piece of shit." Sean pulled the cord again.

Jamie turned his head to look back at him and he frowned. "Problems?"

"Nothing serious," Sean grunted as he pulled the cord a third time. "This bitch is just a bit stubborn."

Raindrops splattered across their skin.

"The storm's here."

"I see that." Sean pulled the cord a fourth time and the motor growled to life. "Finally. Let's get back to shore."

"Good plan."

The growing waves crashed against the bow of the boat, splashing both men with cold water.

"This isn't as much fun as it was," Jamie called out over the combined sound of the wind and the motor.

"I know." Sean tried to spot the cove nearest to where they'd set up their camp. "I know." The wind was blowing more strongly now. *It came up out of nowhere.* It was cold against his rain-soaked skin.

The boat hit another wave.

"You can swim, right?"

Jamie looked back at him. "Yep...can you?" He was holding tightly to the sides of the boat.

"Of course I can." Sean kept a firm grip on the motor. "I think I see our cove."

"It all looks the same to me!"

The boat hit another wave and flipped.

* * *

The two men splashed towards shore, through the shallows with the lake usually only reaching their mid-thighs. Some of the waves, however, soaked them to their chests and almost knocked them from their feet.

Jamie was cursing softly as he looked at the cliffs. The limestone towered well over their heads.

The rain was beating down on them, but given how soaked they already were from their swim through the lake, the rain actually felt warm.

"We need to find shelter." Sean stumbled on a submerged rock, but luckily Jamie was close enough to steady him so that he didn't fall. "I don't think I can find the tent in this weather."

"So a cave then?"

"Or some tree branches. Should be somewhere we can take cover."

"We can't climb that cliff face," Jamie argued. "Not in this rain."

"I know." Sean gestured towards the east. "Keep going that way."

"Which way."

"To your right."

"Are you sure?"

"Yes." Sean splashed through the water. He wished it was light so he could see his footing. *Too shallow to easily swim, to deep to easily walk.*

Jamie followed after him.

He's not complaining at least. Sean laughed.

"Care to share the joke?"

"I was just thinking that I've never had this happen to me before."

"What, getting caught in the rain?"

"No, having the boat flip and sink. I've been caught in the rain before. No big deal...we'll dry out." He looked up at the cliffs. "Eventually."

"I think I see a slope."

"Where?"

"Over there." Jamie pointed. "We might be able to climb it."

"Let's go and try."

It was quite a struggle, but they managed to scramble up the slope. Thick bracken tried to block their way, but they kept forcing their way through it, and finally, they were able to push their way past.

"Over there!" Sean pointed. "A cave."

"Some *cave*."

Sean agreed with the sound of Jamie's disgust.

It was barely more than an outcropping of limestone, with the softer rock underneath worn away by years of erosion. The hollow was only a few square metres, but it was large enough for Sean and Jamie to get out of the rain.

Jamie looked out at the rain. "I'm glad we're out of that pisser." He rubbed his arms. "We need to get warmed up though."

"Yeah, I know." Sean was patting his pockets. "It's times like this that I wished I smoked." He pulled a soaked matchbox from his jeans and grimaced. "These sure as hell aren't gonna light."

"Good thing I come prepared." Jamie was holding a lighter in his hand.

"You smoke?"

"No, but I've gone fishing before. Matches are too unreliable if you get splashed." He looked around. "Any dry wood we can use?"

Sean was already gathering together some branches from beneath a large pine. "This should be dry enough." The ground under the pine was dry. The needles were dry and would make excellent kindling.

The fire crackled and smoked, but it gave off a nice warm.

"We should get out of these wet things. They'll dry better if we hang them up—keep them from chilling us down." Sean licked his lips. "There's no one around to see us. No time to be shy."

"Nope. I've never been a shy lad." Jamie lifted his soaked tee-shirt over his head and wrung it out as best he could.

Sean unbuttoned his short-sleeved shirt and hung it over a pine branch, hoping it would be close enough to the fire to dry. And that the rest of the tree would be enough to keep more rain from falling on it. He undid the Velcro straps on his sneakers and pulled them off.

Jamie was staring out towards the choppy lake. He stood by the fire, shirtless, with the wind ruffling his hair.

Sean couldn't help but stare. *He looks really nice from behind.*

Then Jamie dropped his hands down to the front of his jeans and pushed them down his legs.

Sean swallowed in a suddenly dry throat.

Jamie's light blue briefs were just as soaked as the rest of him was. The thin cotton clung tightly to his groin and butt, leaving hardly anything to Sean's feverish imagination.

So far Jamie appeared to be oblivious to the fact that Sean was staring at his impromptu strip-tease. "I wonder if the storm is going to get any worse," he said. He calmly hung his wet jeans over a tree branch.

"I hope there's no lightning. I'd hate to end this trip by being struck by lightning."

"No, we certainly don't want to get struck," Sean agreed. The front of his own jeans were showing quite the bulge now and he only hoped it would go away before Jamie saw it. *Now is* not *the time!* he thought.

"It feels better to get those wet things off," Jamie commented. "The fire is really nice too." He turned around. "Now I won't die of pneumonia," he said smiling. He was looking at Sean quite openly.

"Good," Sean replied. He licked his lips nervously.

"So...you gonna strip to your underdaks or just stand there and shiver?"

Sean gave a start. "Oh yeah. Course I'm going to finish." His hands dropped down to his fly. He undid his jeans and let them drop. He hung them over tree branch, like Jamie had done, and tried to ignore the fact that he was only wearing grey boxer-briefs. *Just like I'm trying to ignore my hard-on.*

"This is a pretty fierce storm."

The rain was coming down even harder now.

"I think we're in for a long night." Sean eyed their fire. "We might have to spend an uncomfortable night here. I'm sorry about this."

"You promised me an adventure," Jamie told him. "Do you hear me complaining?"

"No, I guess not."

"Reminds me of a camping trip I went on as a kid. A buddy and me got lost in the outback for a few days. Blooming hot sun, scorching temperatures. Nasty."

The absurdity of their situation made Sean laugh. Two grown men, wearing just their underwear, crouching by a fire under a tree in a rainstorm.

Isn't this how you wanted him? a voice asked in his thoughts. *Now you get to have him all to yourself. Half-naked at least, if not drunk.*

Sean sighed. *It's going to be a long night,* he thought. *A long hard night.*

Chapter Twelve

Morning came and Sean opened his eyes. He was laying, curled into a foetal position. He was tenting out the front of his boxer-briefs with an erection harder than any he could recently recall.

Jamie was pressing against his back, his own body mimicking Sean's contours.

And Jamie was sporting his own serious hard-on inside his briefs.

Sean sighed—there was no mistaking the feeling. *Fuck, do I want to take advantage of that piece of meat,* he thought. *Mine and his alike.*

It was torture having to leave it alone.

Sean sighed softly. *Fuck...*

Jamie mumbled something under his breath.

Sean frowned. He shifted position slightly. *That's better.* Jamie's dick was pressing against his ass-crack now. Ever so slowly, every so gently, Sean moved his hips so that he could feel Jamie's hard-on rubbing against his ass.

Two pieces of cotton separate us...might as well be armour plating. Sean suppressed another sigh. He stopped moving. *I don't want him to wake up and find me humping him...or being humped by him. I have to behave myself.*

Which totally sucked.

"Morning."

"Morning." Sean rolled over, moving a bit further away from Jamie. Sometime, despite having a desperately hard erection—and a similar one rubbing against his ass—he'd fallen asleep again. *And our erections have gone down.* That would just have been far too awkward to explain. *Morning wood, gotta love it.* "At least the sun is up."

Jamie had stood up. The front of his briefs were well packed, even with him flaccid. He stretched out his arms and then reached for his jeans. He gave a good shake to loosen them back up, before slowly hauling them up his legs. "You think you can find our way back to camp?"

"Of course, I can." Sean quickly pulled his own jeans on, before he could start growing hard again, then began to button up his shirt. "It shouldn't be too far."

"You think we can find the boat?"

"Maybe. If not, it's not the end of the world."

"You're taking it well."

Sean shrugged. "I got it second hand from a yard sale three years ago. Certainly got way more than my money's worth from it since then."

"Oh, all right then."

* * *

The two men stumbled back into their deserted campsite.

"Looks like everything is still here."

"Yeah." Jamie nodded his own head in agreement. "I need a coffee so badly right now." He paced towards the fire pit and studied the wood already stacked in it. "You want to go and fill the kettle?"

"Most of it looks wet," Sean commented. "We might need to gather some dryer stuff to make a fire."

"I know a few tricks. I think I can get this bastard lit."

"Okay."

Sean reached for the kettle and took a few steps towards the stream. He stopped in his tracks and then glanced back towards the stone-ringed fire pit.

Jamie was bent over the small pit, breaking branches into smaller pieces and laying them loosely. His faded jeans were stretched tightly against his butt.

Sean couldn't help but stare. *It's such a nice sight,* he thought.

Jamie turned around and looked at him.

Sean knew that he had been caught staring.

"You forget where the stream is?" Jamie asked.

"No," Sean replied, somewhat clumsily. "It's just that—" He fell silent as Jamie abandoned the fire pit and walked closer to him.

"You want something from me?" he demanded.

Sean was staring into Jamie's eyes.

"You want the same thing you wanted first thing this morning?"

"Uh—"

Jamie leaned forward, still staring at Sean, and then slowly pressed his lips against the other man's.

Sean hastily pulled him closer, savouring that sensuous kiss. He felt closer to Jamie at that moment than he had ever felt to anyone before. A strong feeling of complete security and peace filled him.

Their kiss was warm and loving. It felt so natural and so right, as if every other kiss in their lives had been done wrong. Their tongues met with a familiarity that was unexplainable, and a passion that was unbelievable.

"Oh, my God, I've waited so long for this," Jamie said softly as he finally exhaled. "I never thought it would happen though."

"I can't believe we didn't see it before. Think of all the wasted time we've got to make up for..." Sean whispered back, still in a state of euphoric shock. "I want you so bad!"

"Fucking A."

With that, they embraced once again, with even more intensity.

They kissed madly, practically swallowing each other's tongues.

Staggering backwards, they tumbled through the tent's flap and inside. They fell onto the mounded sleeping bag without a break in the kissing and finally came to rest with Jamie on his knees, straddling over Sean.

Jamie pushed himself up with his arms and gazed down at Sean's face in a way that melted Sean's soul.

Sean reached down to Jamie's waist and slowly slid his hands up under his tee-shirt. He took his time, allowing his hands to carefully caress the smooth torso and chest, before he finally lifted the tee-shirt up and over his head.

Jamie backed away just long enough to finish removing his tee-shirt, freeing his arms from the sleeves. "My turn," he said softly. His fingers began unbuttoning Sean's shirt.

Sean sat up and allowed Jamie to slide the shirt down his arms. He also took the opportunity to move his head closer to Jamie's chest. His lips closed on the hard nipple.

Jamie inhaled sharply.

Sean smiled. The look on Jamie's face broadcast his emotions perfectly—there was no mistaking his enjoyment. Sean sucked his nipple gently, at least at first, then more with more passionate, biting it ever so teasingly with his front teeth.

Jamie continued to gasp and moan.

Finally, Sean let the nipple slip from his lips with a slurping sound. He kept his tongue extended, and began to work his way downwards along Jamie's chest. He savoured the feeling of the man's soft and smooth skin. Reaching his naval, Sean looked into his eyes.

Jamie was staring back. "Don't stop," he begged.

I'm not turning back now. With that thought, Sean unbuttoned the front of Jamie's *Levi's* and slid them down Jamie's thighs.

Jamie's cock was hard as a rock, bulging out the front of his briefs. He rolled over on his back, just long enough to help finish removing his jeans completely.

Sean gently slid his hand over the other man's crotch and massaged his dick through the thin cotton.

Jamie was practically writhing in a mixture of ecstasy and anticipation.

Sean couldn't wait any longer.

Neither, apparently, could Jamie. At the same moment Sean grabbed the waistband of his briefs, Jamie lifted his ass up just enough to allow the blue briefs to be pulled down and then completely off.

Open-mouthed, Sean stared down at what had to be the most beautiful erection he had ever seen. The perfectly rounded, mushroom head was almost purple in colour, which was contrasted by the peach-toned shaft. His mouth watered intensely as he made my way towards what promised to be a delicious treat.

Lost entirely to desire, Sean slipped the head of Jamie's cock past his lips and into his mouth. He teased the tip of it with his tongue.

Just for a moment, Jamie's whole body stiffened, but then he relaxed again on the sleeping bags.

Sean was keeping track of how Jamie reacted, and he quickly repeated his tongue's movements. He was surprised to realize that he had taken all of Jamie into his mouth. Every inch.

Sean loved the feeling of Jamie's balls gently rubbing against his chin. He inhaled deeply. The scent—the musk—of Jamie was just that intoxicating.

"Christ, mate, you're bloody amazing," Jamie moaned.

Sean pulled his head back, allowing most of Jamie's shaft to emerge from his mouth, before he quickly devoured it again. It was only a matter of a few seconds before Jamie tensed up again and Sean knew that he was very close to reaching his goal.

"Fuck, mate, I-I'm gonna..."

Sean managed a grin, and increased the pressure he was exerting on Jamie's cock.

Jamie's entire body stiffened, and then he arched his back and hips upwards, pushing his cock as far into Sean's throat as he could. "Uunnngh!" he screamed.

Sean was caught off-guard by both the ear-piercing scream and the waves of hot cum suddenly pouring down his throat. *Jamie is shooting gallons!*. He swallowed as fast as he could, but there was too much. Some of the cum was leaking past his lips and dribbling back down Jamie's shaft and onto his beautiful round balls.

Finally, Jamie's spasms subsided and his body went completely limp.

Sean crawled back up, away from his dick, past his firm abs, and then past his chest to his gorgeous lips where this adventure had all begun. He slid his tongue into Jamie's mouth with no resistance.

"Jesus...do you think the park wardens heard you yelling?" Sean asked with a grin.

"Who gives a fuck?" Jamie replied, slumping backwards in exhaustion. His eyes had closed and he exhaled loudly.

Sean snuggled against him. "Do you always scream that loudly?"

"No..."

Is that a blush colouring his cheeks? Sean ran his fingers along Jamie's chest.

Jamie's softening dick twitched. "Stop that."

"Why should I?"

Jamie's eyes opened. "I felt you earlier this morning," Jamie told him softly. "I woke up and you were snoring. You were rock-hard, too."

"Yeah, well was it any wonder?" Sean countered. "I had your hunky body pressing against me." *Just like this.* "All night long, for my mind to dream about."

"You got me so hard—especially when you were rubbing against me like that. I was afraid that you would wake up before I could get myself to go limp again."

"You should've jerked yourself off."

"I thought about it. But moving away from you might have woken you up. And then I'd have to explain this."

"Maybe not." *If I woken up to see you jerking off, I might have thought I was still dreaming.* He had his own hard-on straining out the front of his boxer-briefs. He snuggled closer to the other man, slowly rubbing his chest and legs against Jamie's body. It felt fabulous.

Sean sighed.

Jamie was snoring.

* * *

Sean yawned and stretched out his arms and legs. He opened his eyes and stared up towards the curved arc the tent made over his head.

"I am so sorry about this morning," Jamie said.

Sean blinked. "Huh, wha?" He rubbed his eyes and looked blearily towards the front of the tent. "What?"

"About falling asleep like that. I should've stayed awake and helped you get off." Jamie was crouching in the entryway, wearing a tight pair of red briefs and a smile. Nothing else.

"It's okay," Sean began, "we were both pretty tired out. Not enough sleep last night. Is that coffee I smell?"

"Yep." Jamie's smile grew bigger. "I thought you might like a mug when you eventually woke up."

Sean accepted the offering and took a long swallow. "God, that is good."

"Well, we missed having some first thing."

"Yeah, I know."

"It's afternoon." Jamie was still crouching there, staring at him.

"What?" Sean looked back at his new-found lover. "What is it?" He was shirtless, but still wearing his jeans and shoes.

"You were great this morning," Jamie finally said.

"Thanks." Sean felt a surge of relief at that and a goofy grin filled his face. "I was a bit afraid," he began.

"Of what?"

"That you were going to say that this morning was a mistake."

"It bloody well wasn't!"

Sean's stomach growled. Loudly.

Jamie was grinning. "I've got a fire going. I'll throw something on for a very late lunch or an even later breakfast. An early supper, if you prefer."

"That would be appreciated." Sean rolled over. "I'll come out and give you a hand in a moment. Just let me find something to put on."

* * *

The two ate their fill.

"Packaged this and dehydrated that..." Jamie shook his head. "This isn't real food."

"It doesn't match the barbeque we had last week," Sean agreed. "But you can't carry a full grocery store with you."

"No, I guess not. Some fresh fish might have been nice."

Sean didn't say anything.

"Shit! Sorry, I forgot that we lost your fishing poles with the boat."

"It's okay." Sean managed a shrug. "They were old. I've been thinking about buying some new gear."

"I'll chip in."

"You don't have too."

"It's the least I can do, mate. You wouldn't have lost them if I hadn't come along."

"Oh, be quiet. Don't worry about it." Sean sipped at his coffee. He found himself staring at Jamie.

Jamie was staring back at him.

And we're just sitting here in our underwear as if that's the normal thing for two guys to do. Sean found that almost absurd, but he was enjoying it. *As long as Jamie doesn't get dressed, I'm not going to either.* Their underwear was every bit as respectable as most bathing suits were.

"I'm thinking about going inside for a bit," Jamie announced. He'd gotten to his feet and vanished into the forest for a few minutes, before returning.

Sean smiled. "Tired already?"

"Not exactly, mate." Jamie had a bright gleam in his eye. "Come over here."

Sean hurried to obey, eager to find out what his friend had planned next.

Inside the tent, Jamie shifted positions on the sleeping bag, sliding and positioning his ass right at the edge, with his legs spread wide open. "I want you to fuck me," he announced simply.

"Right here? Right now?"

"Yeah."

"Are you sure about that?"

"Damn right I am, mate. There's a tube of *KY* in the top flap of my pack." He hooked his thumb towards it.

Yes! Sean hurried to it and pulled the flap open. He removed the tube—it was cool to his fevered touch—and just as quickly scurried back to Jamie's side. He dropped to his knees, flipped up the top on the lube and squeezed a generous helping into the palm of his hand.

Jamie spread his legs even more. "Do it."

Sean smeared the lube around the beckoning hole. "I'll be gentle." He slowly eased his index finger inside, to better help prepare Jamie for what was coming next.

Jamie groaned.

A smile played on Sean's lips. He slid his finger in and out, the rhythm of a simulated fuck. *He's accommodating this really easily...he's no virgin.*

"Put another one in," Jamie pleaded. "It feels so good!"

On the next stroke, Sean inserted his middle finger alongside his index finger.

Jamie twitched, but quickly relaxed. "Oh, yeah..." he exhaled, signalling his approval.

Sean's hard-on had stiffened fully to attention, and he was eager to take full advantage of the offered hole. *After so much body contact already between us, I couldn't possibly resist!* He slowly pulled his fingers out, feeling Jamie's ass contracting as if to keep them from going.

Jamie shifted positions, lifting both of his legs until they rested on Sean's shoulders.

Sean quickly squeezed more lube out and applied it to his throbbing cock. He was resting the tip against Jamie's ass. "Ready yourself," he prompted.

Jamie bared his teeth. "Stop arseing around and shove it in!"

Sean pressed against him firmly and forced the mushroom-shaped head inside Jamie's ass.

Jamie gasped, a quick intake of breath, his entire body tensing, until the initial pain subsided.

"Are you okay?" Sean asked him. "I can pull out."

"Don't you fucking dare!" Jamie replied hungrily. "Slowly, though."

Sean slowly allowed his throbbing prick to inch its way deeper into Jamie's tight ass. The sensations he felt were incredible. The other man's hot, tight ass hole was like a sheath of velvet tightly wrapped around his cock, the muscles massaging it gently.

Finally, Sean had given him all that he had to give—he could feel his pubes brushing against Jamie's balls. Holding him with one hand on each of his hips, Sean slowly pulled back out, leaving just the tip inside. Then, with a bit more force than the first time, he plunged all the way back in.

"Oh, God yes!" Jamie cried out. "Fuck me!" he whimpered pleadingly.

Sean pulled out again and then began ramming him with all his might! He pulled Jamie towards his with each thrust, causing their bodies to slap against each other with a smacking sound. He could feel his orgasm building in his balls, which were now tingling with the need to cum.

Jamie's own dick had grown hard again, and he was stroking it madly in time with my pumping.

"Uuuhhhh!" Sean grunted as he clenched his teeth, trying not to scream out from the ecstasy he was feeling. "Oh, God, yes...." He continued pounding away, each stroke bringing him closer to the brink.

"Aaahhhhhhhhh!" Jamie's orgasm began with a squirt that splashed white goop across his own chin.

Jamie blowing his load all over himself was enough to finally push Sean over the edge. The sight of his friend cumming, added to the strong sensations of Jamie's ass muscles tightening around his dick with each spasm of his cock, and Sean couldn't hang back.

Sean's creamy spunk erupted as forcefully as his own pent-up cry of release. He shot his load deep into his partner's bowels...and that was enough to trigger yet another volley of cum to shoot out of Jamie's semi-hard dick.

The cycle fed back and Sean continued to shoot his load.

After what surely must have been the longest—and what certainly was the most intense—orgasm of his entire life, Sean collapsed on top of Jamie. His gradually softening dick slid out of the well-lubricated hole with a soft pop.

Jamie groaned and let his legs thump back onto the ground.

Sean could feel cum leaking past his dick and running down the inside of Jamie's thighs. He gently kissed Jamie's chest and nipples as both men attempted to catch their breath.

"You are bloody amazing, mate." Jamie was laying there on the sleeping bag with his eyes half-closed. "I had no idea you were this good."

"You're not half bad yourself."

"I should've jumped you first thing this morning. Hell, I should've jumped you the first day we met."

"I've wanted you since then too."

Jamie's eyes opened. "You calling it love at first sight?"

Sean shook his head. "I'm not sure about 'love'. 'Lust' certainly."

Jamie chuckled. "Lust at first sight...that's a new one."

Chapter Thirteen

"I think your sleeping bag is ruined."

Sean opened his eyes. "Sorry? What did you say?"

Jamie was crouching beside him. He was dressed in just his briefs. "I said 'I think your sleeping bag is ruined'. Or badly stained at the very least."

"Oh, we made a bit of a mess." Sean stared at the stain marks. *Did we ever make a mess!* "I must've shot a lot."

"Yep, you did at that." Jamie gave his head a shake. "I can still feel it." He shifted positions slightly and tried to wipe dried cum from his inner thigh.

Sean sat up. "It'll wash out. Or not." He wasn't particularly concerned. *Not after we had such wonderful sex.* Three or four times during the night...at least. *I lost track of just how many times we fucked. Hell, I lost track of the* year *during all that.*

"And what about me?"

"We'll just have to wash you too."

Sean and Jamie headed for the stream.

The two men were wearing their underwear. Officially it was to provide some dignity in case anyone stumbled across their campsite.

But I think it's only adding to the erotic nature of this, Sean thought. He could only admire the manner in which the light blue briefs clung to Jamie's body. *A lot nicer than any* Speedo.

Jamie, for his part, seemed to equally enjoy the sight of the boxer-briefs Sean was wearing. "They look comfy enough," he'd said, "but I bet you'd look hot in a pair of these daks."

The two men waded into the cool water.

"That feels so good," Jamie said.

Sean had a bar of soap in his hand. He dunked it in the stream, and then began to work it across his chest.

"We should see about getting you cleaned up," Sean said. He reached his soapy hands inside Jamie's briefs and started stroking his rapidly hardening cock. "Yes, I think I can get all of this monster clean."

"Oh, God, mate!"

Sean pulled the briefs down, so that waistband was resting under Jamie's balls. He kept stroking Jamie's raging hard-on.

"Fuck!" Jamie grunted.

Sean felt hot cum splash across his chest. "Wow."

"I don't usually have distance," Jamie gasped.

Sean wiped his hand off on his own chest. "I'll clean it later."

"We can do it now," Jamie told him.

* * *

Sean stared at the house across the driveway. Following their return to the city, Jamie had vanished inside and he hadn't seen him since.

Was what happened between on us the camping trip a mistake? Sean hoped not. *I don't want to lose his friendship.*

Sean paced to the washing machine as it buzzed. He pulled the sleeping bag out and stuffed it into the dryer.

He just said that he was going to go and check his phone messages, Sean thought as he stared through the window. *How long does that take?* He shook his head. He still hadn't gotten around to checking his own machine for any messages. And he certainly wasn't taking a cell-phone with him on a camping trip.

"Never anything good," he muttered aloud. Just telemarketers.

Who might have called him? His friend from the rainstorm? Sean frowned. *Maybe they really are an item. I could've just been a one night stand.*

A part of him had to admit that if he was just a one night stand, then at least he'd had *that* one night.

He did live up to my fantasies, Sean admitted. *He was great.* And those memories would spawn a hundred fantasy sessions.

"But I'd rather have the real thing," he said.

* * *

"So how was the camping weekend?" Jackie asked. "Did you get rained out?"

"We survived the storm," Sean told her as he refilled his coffee mug. "Got a bit wet, of course, but that's all part of the fun."

"Some *fun.*"

"You have no idea what it was like."

"Huddling around a campfire for warmth. Swatting at mosquitoes and bugs." Jackie managed a rather theatrical shudder. "No thank you. Give me a luxury hotel anytime."

"It was a fun weekend."

"Did you catch anything?"

"A few trout. We let them go though...not big enough to be worth eating."

"So hours in a boat, sitting and doing nothing, and you have nothing to show for it?" Jackie shook her head again. "You are crazy."

"It's the thrill of the hunt," Sean told her. "Like when you go looking for a new pair of shoes."

She looked at him, her eyes narrowing. "I do not obsess over shoes," she said. "I do not spend hours and hours looking in different stores and trying on numerous pairs."

"Oh no, of course you don't." Sean failed to stifle his laughter.

Jackie sniffed.

"Have either of you seen Eric?" Sylvester asked as he stuck his head into the office.

"No, not so far."

"Yeah," Sean said. "I've not yet had the pleasure of a royal visit."

"He's furious." Sylvester was chuckling. "The hotel lost his reservation so he had got stuck in a small room. A waiter spilled wine on his tan suit at dinner—the dry cleaner couldn't get the stain out. His car got dinged in the parking lot at some point—and the hotel won't pay for repairs."

"Oh, poor Eric."

"Poor us!" Jackie exclaimed. "Think about it, Sean. He's going to be on a rampage about this for days. Weeks."

"That's not the best part of the story."

"It's not?"

"No, Jackie…he dressed up in his ritzy clothes and went to a bar and tried to pick up a girl. Her boyfriend wasn't too pleased with that."

Sean winced. "How badly was he hurt?"

Sylvester waved his hand dismissively. "The boyfriend and his buddies—a charming gay couple from what I've heard—took exception to his tone. He insinuated that he was a better class of person than she was likely to find there. Made a few other comments about his bedroom prowess and how fancy his car was. She slapped him so he cursed her out. The other three gentlemen then dragged him to the bathroom. He later left the bar in just a pair of extremely short cut-offs and his shoes. Nothing else."

"And he told you all this?"

"Of course not. Not about the bar incident at least. Ann-Marie was there. You remember her from Boretsky's?"

The other two nodded.

"Well, she was attending the conference for their firm. She was at the bar and saw everything. She even got part of it recorded on her cell-phone. Mostly Eric being dragged off by two obvious queens and then his later attempt to slink out of the bar without anyone noticing his jeans and shirt had been ripped off."

"You have pictures?"

"Video."

Sean laughed. "Can we see this?"

* * *

"G'day, mate! Look, I'm really sorry for ignoring you like that." Jamie was clean-shaven, aside from his usual moustache, and his tee-shirt and shorts were equally clean. "I got tied up on the phone the other night. My mother called from home and wanted to tell me everything I've missed. She likes to talk and talk and talk...I thought I'd never get away."

"Not a problem." Sean gave him a smile as he stepped away from his car. A clean and smiling Jamie had come hurrying over to him as soon as he had begun pulling into the driveway. *He was obviously watching for me to come home.* "I just figured you were busy with something."

"Well, I was. One thing led to another and I never seemed able to get away to come back across the street."

"It's okay. After the trip, I had to tidy up and do laundry and stuff."

"I should've been there to help you," Jamie said. He had stuffed his hands into the back pockets of his shorts. "I helped make the *mess* after all."

Sean chuckled.

"I wanted to come back over, but you never seem to be home when I am. Work's been running late lately."

I noticed you weren't coming back after dark, Sean thought, but he didn't say anything. *I thought you doing it so you could ignore me.*

"We just fell behind some they've been pushing the overtime to try and get the job back on schedule. Even before all that rain last week, we were behind. The rains just made it that much worse. Course, the overtime pay is real nice."

"That should help get your bills caught up."

"I don't have many bills. I live cheap. Just food and gas mostly. Jacob won't take more than a pittance for my staying with him."

"You'll have a fortune saved up in no time then." Sean chuckled. "I could give you some accounting advice and you could retire early."

"I've got plenty of cash already," Jamie told him. "I didn't come over here to live on the sweat of others. I planned to work hard. I do work hard." He paused for a moment. "I'm saving up for my own place."

"You're going to buy a house?"

"Why not? Bloody hell, mate, I might just hire myself to help build one." Jamie laughed loudly.

Sean joined in. "I've heard worse ideas."

"In the meantime, though, I plan to enjoy my cash. We all knocked off the job early today—waiting for supplies to arrive before we can do more—and I took advantage of it. I was really hoping to see you today. I wanted to get some grub in and have you over for supper. My way of thanking you for a fun weekend away."

"Even with everything?"

"Even with the sinking of our boat and the night huddled in the rain." Jamie's smile was getting bigger. "It's the fun stuff that make a trip memorable."

"It definitely was memorable," Sean agreed.

"So, how about you come over tonight for supper?" Jamie asked. "I've got some chops for the barbie and some salad. Got some alcohol in too—I fancied these drinks a mate of mine used to make so I laid in the mixings."

"I think I can come over, though I do have to work tomorrow."

"Go and get cleaned up and change into something comfortable." Jamie gave him a wink. "Though you do look fucking hot in that suit."

"Thanks." Sean nodded. "I'll grab a shower and then come and join you."

"All right, I'll have everything ready." Jamie waved. "See you."

Sean went inside.

His phone was flashing.

He hit the *play* button and then poured himself some juice from the fridge.

"*So, did you take my advice?*" Rosemary's voice asked. "*Have you gotten him drunk yet? Is he any good in bed? Did you have to use the too-much alcohol excuse? Do you have pictures? Talk to me, luv, talk to me!*"

Chuckling, Sean just shook his head.

"I should call her," he thought, "but I'm just not in the mood." The camping trip had been amazing, all things considered, and now he was looking forward to seeing what else might come from it.

"Or is our friendship over and done?" That was his biggest fear. "Are we starting something new...or is this going to be like the expression 'what happens in Vegas, stays in Vegas'?"

Chapter Fourteen

"We can drink to celebrate our safe return!" Jamie declared as he handed Sean a drink. "You need to try this. A little mix a buddy of mine made for us at beach parties back in Bondi. A couple of these and you're ready to go surfing with the sharks." He laughed.

Dressed in loose shorts and an equally loose tee-shirt, Sean sniffed at the glass.

"Go on, chug it back." Jamie held his own glass to his mouth. "You always chug the first one." He followed his own advice.

Smoke puffed from the barbeque.

"Those chops should be done soon." Jamie walked towards the barbeque. "I got us some of the best lamb I could see. The trick is cooking it just enough...you still want it pink inside."

"I've been told that."

"The spice rub is my own invention."

"Did you tell the butcher you were going to rub the chops?"

"Yeah. The clerk laughed and suggested something with a bone to make it better. It was that cute blond—the one you like eying so much."

"Ah." Sean finished his drink. It was strong, but flavourful.

Jamie refilled his glass. "Have another, mate." He raised his own glass. "To good neighbours."

"And better friends."

* * *

Sean blinked, strained to bring the world into focus.

As he looked around the bedroom, he realized that he wasn't in his own bed. *Where am I?* he had to wonder. The furniture was the wrong colour and the ceiling fan slowly turning overhead was not the one he had installed.

Hearing a snore, he turned to his right.

Jamie was laying in bed beside him, still sleeping peacefully—the sheet was down around his waist, and his smooth bare chest rising and falling slowly with the pace of his breathing.

He looks as happy as I feel, Sean thought. *It's not a dream...this is real!*

Not wanting to wake his lover, Sean slowly moved to the edge of the queen-sized bed and climbed out.

He stared at his reflection in the mirror. He was naked and his morning hard-on was standing almost at full attention. He could see Jamie laying in the bed, past his shoulder.

Sean was sticky, with dried cum on his stomach and legs. *What all did we get up too last night?* He couldn't recall the entire evening. *How much did I drink?*

With a grunt, he headed for the bathroom. He turned on the shower and stared at his reflection in the mirror over the sink while the water heated up.

Steam was starting to billow past the shower curtain.

Sean allowed himself to smile in anticipation. He was really looking forward to a nice hot shower—and the steam meant this one was ready. He reached for the controls and adjusted the temperature to be a bit cooler and then he stepped under the spray.

He sighed as the warm water ran down his entire body. It felt really good, just standing there and rinsing away yesterday in preparation for today.

And it's going to be a very good day, Sean thought to himself. *After all, the objection of months of my wild fantasizing is asleep in the next room!* He squeezed some shampoo into his hand and began to massage it into his hair. With his eyes tightly closed, he began rinsing it out when a hand gently caressed his back.

"G'day, mate." Jamie's voice was unmistakable.

Just that simple little touch was more than enough to send blood rushing into Sean's dick and it sprang to full attention. Within seconds, he was rock-hard.

"Wow, that popped up quick," Jamie commented.

"What can I say—you do have that effect on me." Sean ducked back under the spray to finish rinsing the shampoo from his hair.

"Good!" replied Jamie.

Sean could hear the other man climbing into the tub.

Jamie continued to massage Sean's shoulders, moving closer as he did so.

"Oh, *God*! Do you *ever* have an effect on me!" Sean repeated.

"You're hot enough to make me burst my daks," Jamie told him.

"I can tell." Sean could feel Jamie's hard-on pressing against his ass.

Sean turned around and his own hard dick bounced against Jamie's.

With the shampoo all rinsed away, Sean was finally able to open his eyes. *Now that really is a fabulous sight for this thing in the morning.*

Jamie looked unbelievable standing there with the water glistening on his smooth, lightly tanned skin.

Sean bent his head forward and kissed him.

Jamie's tongue darted into his mouth.

Sean slid his hands down Jamie's back, coming to rest on his ass-cheeks. He used his grip to pull the other man closer, thrusting his own hips forward to maximize the contact and pressure between their slippery bodies.

Jamie responded by thrusting his own hips, forcing his hard cock to slid up and down against Sean's leg, and at the same time massaging Sean's dick against his abdomen.

"Mmm, that feels good," Sean gasped.

Jamie shifted positions, moving himself more under the spray, and also pressing even more tightly against Sean.

Sean pulled back so that he could admire the sight of the water flowing down across Jamie's chest, dripping from the end of his hard-on, and running down his legs.

"You like what you see?"

"Yeah." He pulled Jamie forward, out of the shower stream. He quickly snatched up the shampoo bottle and squeezed some into his hand. He began to gently lather up the other man's head.

There was an amused smile playing across Jamie's face as Sean massaged his scalp. He had closed his eyes.

Sean once again pulled him, back into the spray so that the water could rinse his hair. At the same time, he began to slowly gyrate his hips, grinding his hard, wet cock against the other man's leg.

Jamie began to moan softly.

Sean reached down and put his hand on the other man's hard-on. He rubbed it with his open palm, dragging his fingers up and down, from tip to balls.

Jamie grunted, his eyes still closed, and he seemed to grow even harder.

Finally, with a big grin, Sean squirted some body-wash gel into his palm and then closed his fingers around the shaft.

"Oh, yeah," Jamie groaned as he felt himself being stroked.

Sean used his grip to slowly turn Jamie towards the wall. He stepped closer, sliding his hard dick in between the other man's ass-cheeks. He kept stroking Jamie's shaft, while sliding his own dick up and down the crack of the other man's ass.

Jamie was groaning.

Sean was really enjoying the sensations as well. He used his free hand to squirt more wash gel onto his chest and his cock.

"Oh, god!" Jamie groaned softly. "Keep doing that."

Sean began sliding his body more quickly across the other man's. The gel made his skin slick and the feel of their slippery bodies against each other felt unbelievably arousing.

"I'm getting close!" Jamie gasped.

"So am—fuck!" Sean felt himself shoot, his own orgasm striking. Spurt after spurt of white cum erupted from his dick, splashing up Jamie's crack and onto his back.

At the same instant, Jamie cried out and Sean's felt the sudden warmth of his lover's cum oozing over his fingers as they gripped his dick.

They stood stiffly for a long moment, breathing heavily, before slowly relaxing in each other's arms.

"Oh my god, mate! That was fucking incredible."

Sean nodded, still speechless.

"I don't know where you learned that trick, but it was great." Jamie reached for the body-wash and the facecloth. "Bloody hell...."

"I think that was even more better than last night," Sean said, finally getting his breath back enough to speak.

"I can't wait for round three then."

"You can't be serious."

"I am...round three later this arvo. Afternoon," he amended as he continued to lather up his chest and arms. "Or this evening."

Sean shook his head tiredly.

"We're both gonna be going in to work bow-legged," Jamie said with a mischievous grin.

Sean shook his head again. *I don't even know what time it is,* he thought. "Aren't we already late?"

"Maybe. Who gives a fuck?" Covered with lather, Jamie turned his attentions to Sean and began to work the soapy cloth across his body.

Sean felt like crawling back into bed and just enjoying the massage. Jamie had worked his way down his body and was playfully soaping up his crotch. "Hey, leave me some skin!" he said.

"Just making sure you're all cleaned up."

Sean flinched as Jamie gave his semi-erect dick a squeeze.

With a reluctant sigh, Jamie wrung the cloth out and hung in back on the rack so they could rinse off.

With similar reluctance, Sean stepped out of the tub and Jamie followed. They took turns towelling each other off.

As Jamie gently dried his back, Sean could see his face in the mirror.

Jamie's expression was one of mingled disbelief, elation, and some confusion all at once.

The same way I feel. Sean turned and let his towel drop to the floor. Jamie opened his mouth.

Without giving him time to fumble for words, Sean pressed his lips against Jamie's. He kissed him slowly and passionately. Breaking lip contact, Sean smiled. "I think I love you."

"So do I," Jamie replied. "You told you this neighbourhood had a lot to offer...and I said I was going to take advantage of everything."

"That you did."

Also by Frank Sol

Novels Of The Sensual City
A Family Affair
Delivering The Goods
Divine Punishment
Good Neighbours
Just Between Friends
Landscaping, Manscaping
Titan's Cradle - A Novel of the Sensual Suns
Terran Cummando - A Novel Of The Sensual Suns

Novels On The Prairies
Bareback Range
Return To Bareback Range
Fenced In